THE STORY SO FAR...

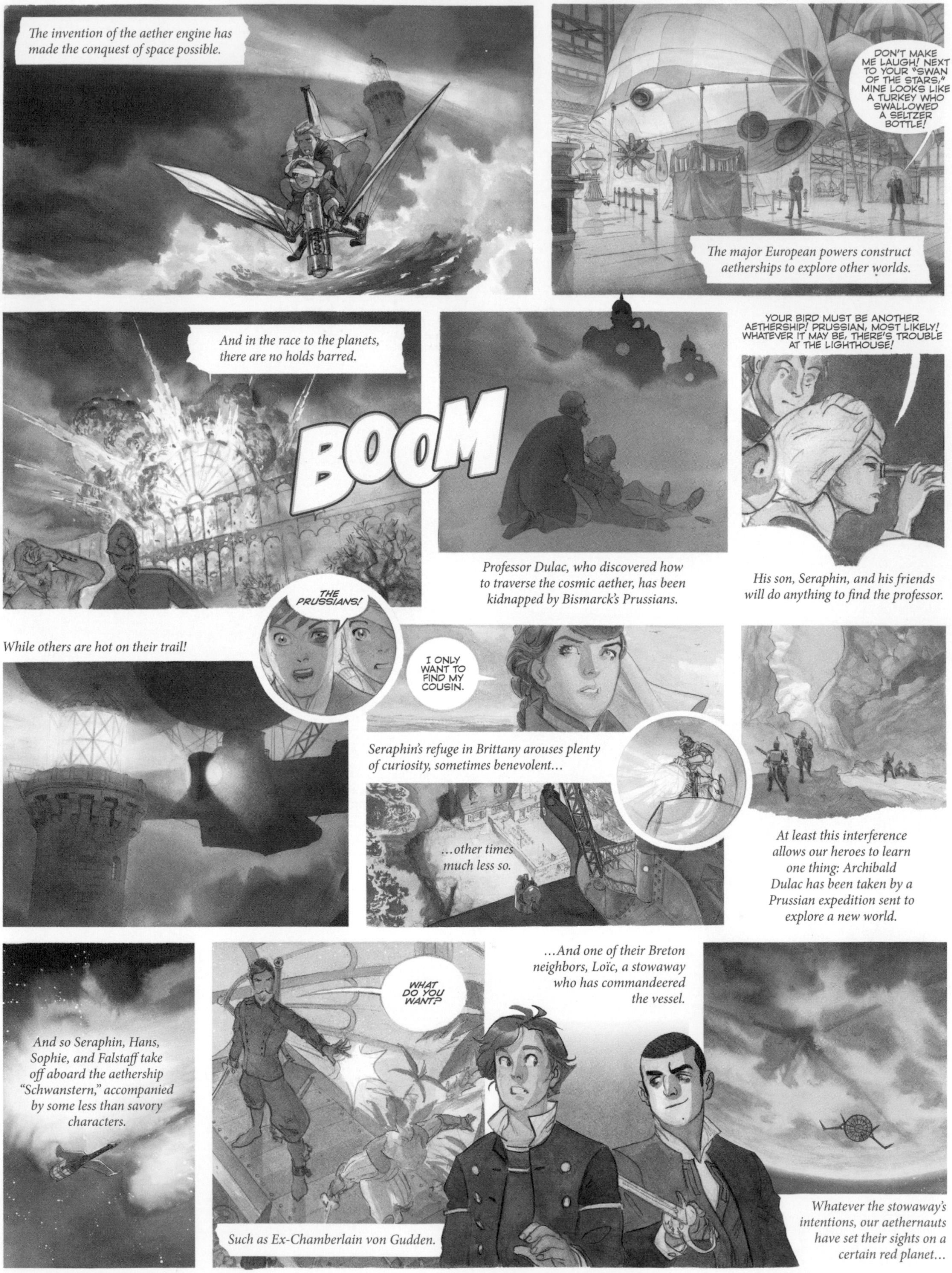
The invention of the aether engine has made the conquest of space possible.
DON'T MAKE ME LAUGH! NEXT TO YOUR "SWAN OF THE STARS," MINE LOOKS LIKE A TURKEY WHO SWALLOWED A SELTZER BOTTLE!
The major European powers construct aetherships to explore other worlds.
And in the race to the planets, there are no holds barred.
BOOM
Professor Dulac, who discovered how to traverse the cosmic aether, has been kidnapped by Bismarck's Prussians.
YOUR BIRD MUST BE ANOTHER AETHERSHIP! PRUSSIAN, MOST LIKELY! WHATEVER IT MAY BE, THERE'S TROUBLE AT THE LIGHTHOUSE!
His son, Seraphin, and his friends will do anything to find the professor.
While others are hot on their trail!
THE PRUSSIANS!
I ONLY WANT TO FIND MY COUSIN.
Seraphin's refuge in Brittany arouses plenty of curiosity, sometimes benevolent...
...other times much less so.
At least this interference allows our heroes to learn one thing: Archibald Dulac has been taken by a Prussian expedition sent to explore a new world.
And so Seraphin, Hans, Sophie, and Falstaff take off aboard the aethership "Schwanstern," accompanied by some less than savory characters.
WHAT DO YOU WANT?
Such as Ex-Chamberlain von Gudden.
...And one of their Breton neighbors, Loïc, a stowaway who has commandeered the vessel.
Whatever the stowaway's intentions, our aethernauts have set their sights on a certain red planet...

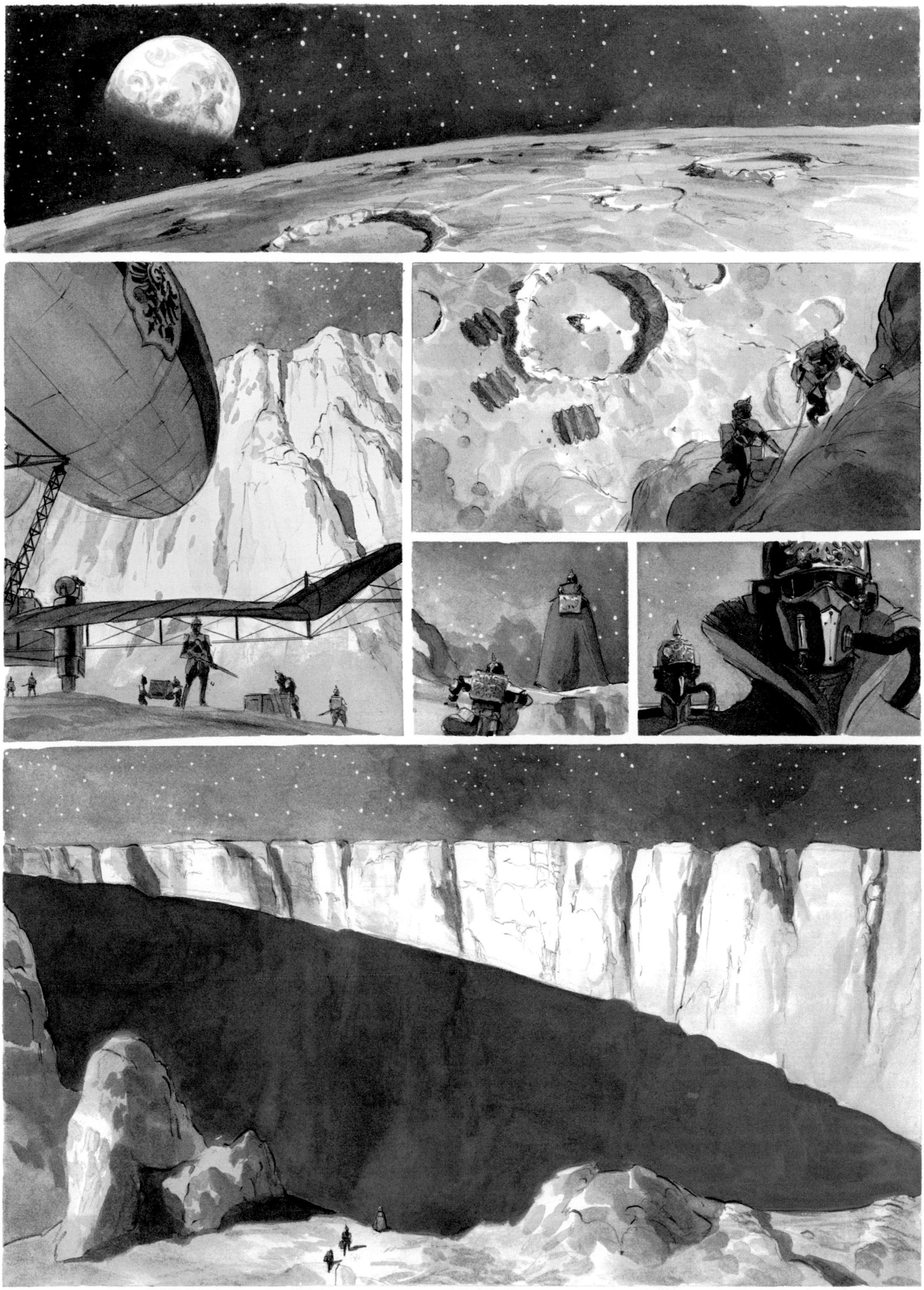

ALEX ALICE

CASTLE
IN
THE
STARS

A FRENCHMAN ON MARS

First Second
New York

First Second

English translation by Anne and Owen Smith
English translation copyright © 2020 by Roaring Brook Press

Published by First Second
First Second is an imprint of Roaring Brook Press,
a division of Holtzbrinck Publishing Holdings Limited Partnership
120 Broadway, New York, NY 10271

Don't miss your next favorite book from First Second! For the latest updates go
to firstsecondnewsletter.com and sign up for our enewsletter.

Library of Congress Control Number: 2019948148

ISBN: 978-1-250-20681-7

Our books may be purchased in bulk for promotional, educational, or business use.
Please contact your local bookseller or the Macmillan Corporate and Premium Sales Department
at (800) 221-7945 ext. 5442 or by email at MacmillanSpecialMarkets@macmillan.com.

First American edition, 2020

American edition edited by Mark Siegel and Bethany Bryan
Interior book design by Chris Dickey

Printed in China by RR Donnelley Asia Printing Solutions Ltd., Dongguan City, Guangdong Province

Originally published in 2018 in French by Rue de Sèvres as *Le château des étoiles — Tome 4: Un français sur Mars*
French text and illustrations by Alex Alice copyright © 2018 by Rue de Sèvres, Paris

10 9 8 7 6 5 4 3 2 1

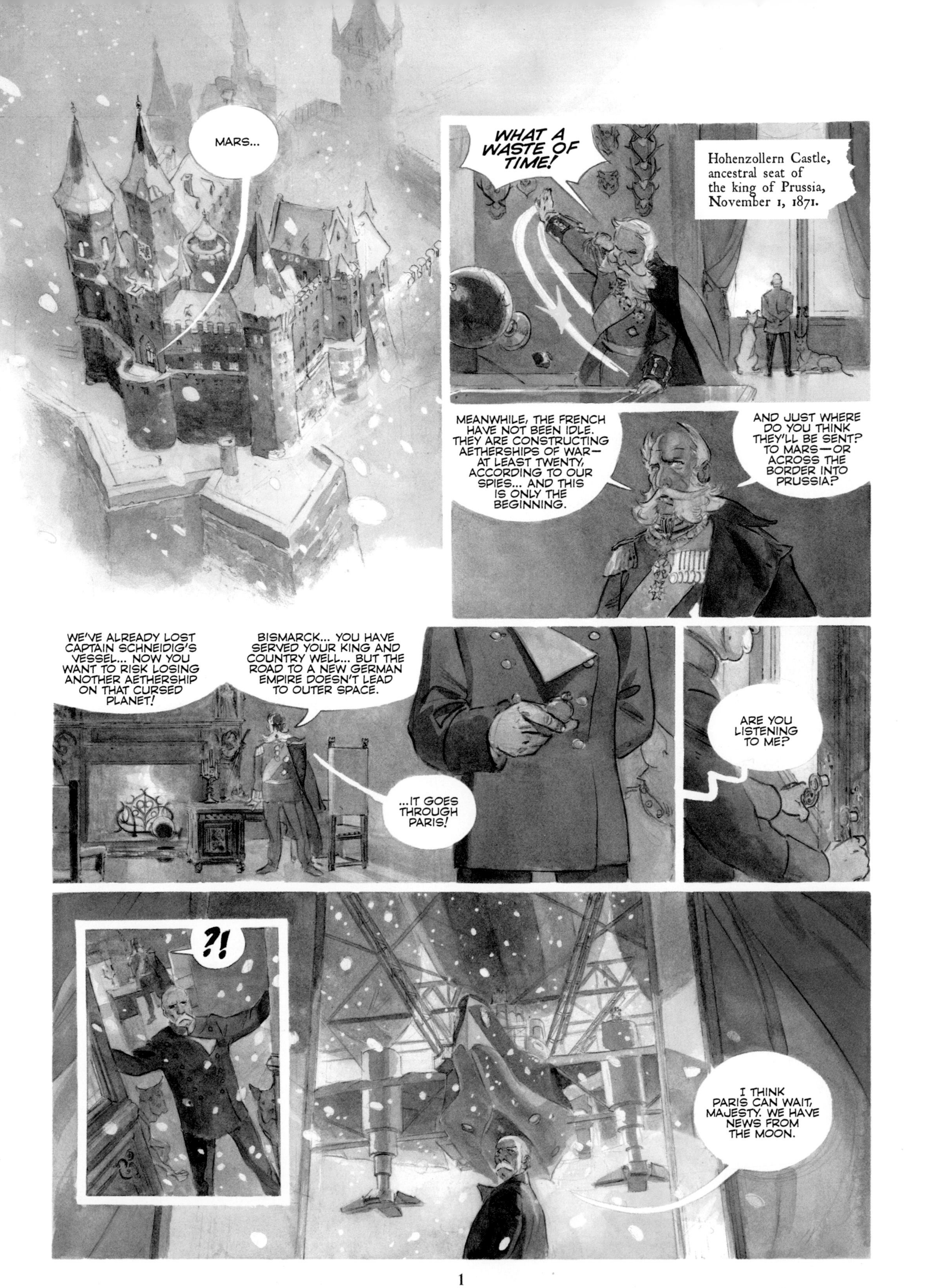
MARS...
WHAT A WASTE OF TIME!
Hohenzollern Castle, ancestral seat of the king of Prussia, November 1, 1871.
MEANWHILE, THE FRENCH HAVE NOT BEEN IDLE. THEY ARE CONSTRUCTING AETHERSHIPS OF WAR—AT LEAST TWENTY, ACCORDING TO OUR SPIES... AND THIS IS ONLY THE BEGINNING.
AND JUST WHERE DO YOU THINK THEY'LL BE SENT? TO MARS—OR ACROSS THE BORDER INTO PRUSSIA?
WE'VE ALREADY LOST CAPTAIN SCHNEIDIG'S VESSEL... NOW YOU WANT TO RISK LOSING ANOTHER AETHERSHIP ON THAT CURSED PLANET!
BISMARCK... YOU HAVE SERVED YOUR KING AND COUNTRY WELL... BUT THE ROAD TO A NEW GERMAN EMPIRE DOESN'T LEAD TO OUTER SPACE.
...IT GOES THROUGH PARIS!
ARE YOU LISTENING TO ME?
?!
I THINK PARIS CAN WAIT, MAJESTY. WE HAVE NEWS FROM THE MOON.

I CAN HARDLY BELIEVE IT... A TOTALLY INVISIBLE ROCK!

AND YOU SAY IT CAME FROM THE MOON?

WE TOOK IT FROM THE SITE OF THE ANOMALY OF MARCH 15, 1870.

IT'S INCREDIBLE...

...BUT PERFECTLY USELESS!

THE EXPERIMENT IS READY, MR. PRIME MINISTER.

?

MAJESTY, IF YOU WOULD BE SO KIND AS TO ACTIVATE THE ELECTRIC FIELD...

CLACK

...

CRUNCH

!

BEHOLD THE OBJECTIVE OF OUR MISSION! THIS IS THE SUBSTANCE THAT ALLOWS PROFESSOR DULAC'S CONTRAPTION TO FLY WITHOUT A BALLOON—AETHERITE!

FROM NOW ON, OUR AERIAL SUPREMACY DEPENDS ENTIRELY ON THIS CRYSTAL!

WHY, THEN, SHOULD WE CONCERN OURSELVES WITH MARS? YOU TOLD ME JUST NOW THAT THIS ROCK WAS FOUND ON THE MOON!

AFTER FOUR MONTHS OF SEARCHING, ADMIRAL HECKS COULD FIND NO OTHER SAMPLE OF THIS SUBSTANCE...

...BUT WE KNOW WHERE TO LOOK!

WE DISCOVERED THESE CHARTS IN CAVES ALONG THE BORDER OF THE LUNAR CRATER.

!

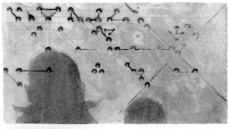

IT LOOKS LIKE...

WRITING.

DO YOU MEAN TO SAY...

THE AETHERITE DID NOT ORIGINATE ON THE MOON...

WHILE WE HAVE YET TO DECIPHER THE ENTIRE INSCRIPTION, WE HAVE IDENTIFIED THE SOURCE OF THE AETHERITE...

2

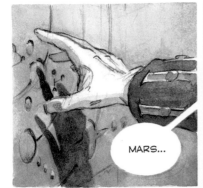

IF MARS HOLDS THE SECRET OF AETHERITE...THEN WHOEVER CONTROLS THE RED PLANET WILL BE THE MASTER OF THE SOLAR SYSTEM...

MARS...

HOW SOON CAN YOU LEAVE?

MR. PRIME MINISTER, PROFESSOR DULAC IS NO LONGER OF ANY USE TO US. WHAT SHALL WE DO WITH HIM?

NEVER FEAR, ADMIRAL...

OUR PRISONER HAS ONE LAST ROLE TO PLAY...

"...WHETHER HE WANTS TO OR NOT!"

CHAPTER 10

A FRENCHMAN ON MARS

EASY DOES IT, SERAPHIN!

HOW DO YOU EXPECT ME TO SPOT THE PRUSSIAN VESSEL WHEN YOU KEEP TOSSING US ABOUT?

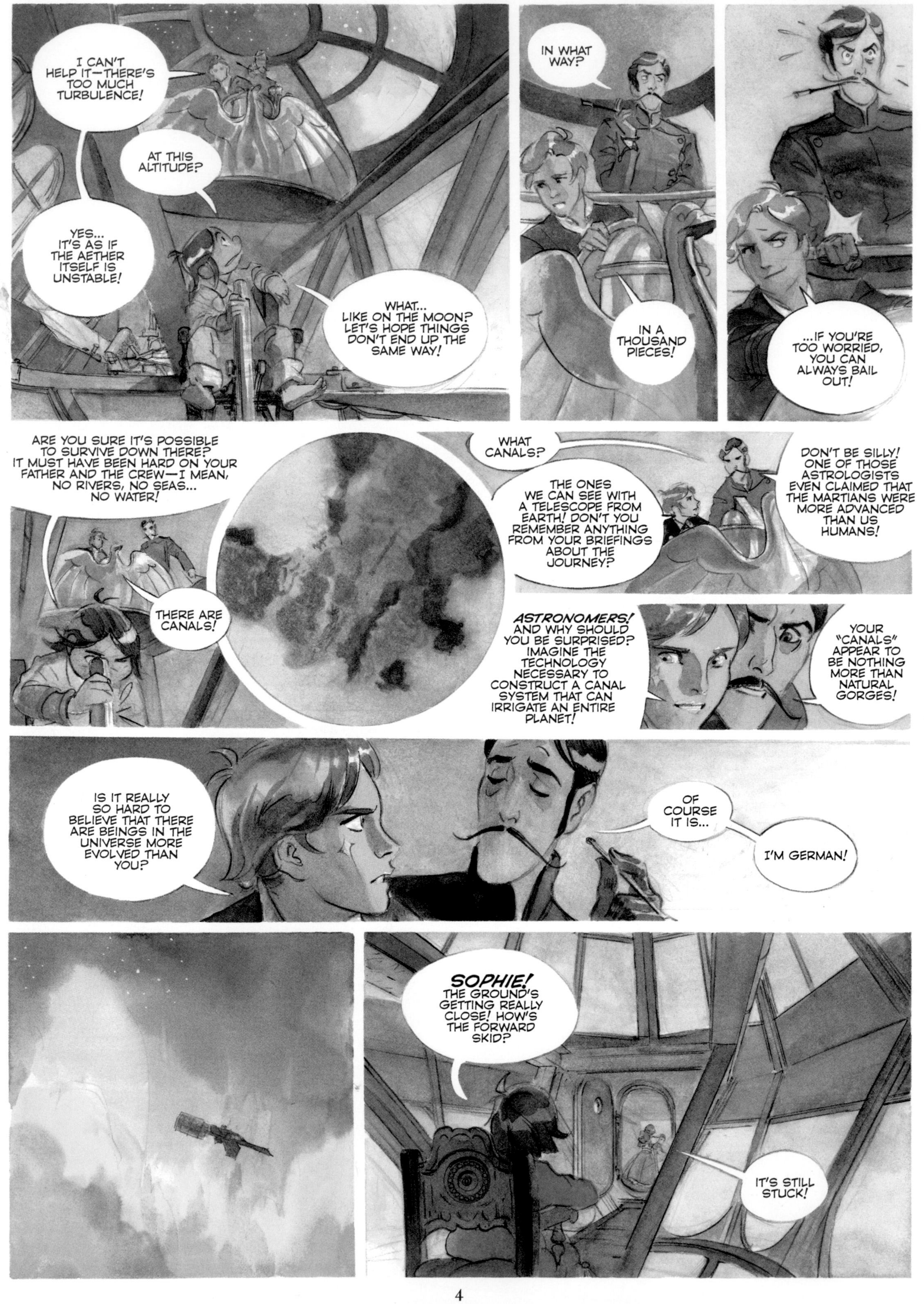
I CAN'T HELP IT—THERE'S TOO MUCH TURBULENCE!
AT THIS ALTITUDE?
YES... IT'S AS IF THE AETHER ITSELF IS UNSTABLE!
WHAT... LIKE ON THE MOON? LET'S HOPE THINGS DON'T END UP THE SAME WAY!
IN WHAT WAY?
IN A THOUSAND PIECES!
...IF YOU'RE TOO WORRIED, YOU CAN ALWAYS BAIL OUT!
ARE YOU SURE IT'S POSSIBLE TO SURVIVE DOWN THERE? IT MUST HAVE BEEN HARD ON YOUR FATHER AND THE CREW—I MEAN, NO RIVERS, NO SEAS... NO WATER!
THERE ARE CANALS!
WHAT CANALS?
THE ONES WE CAN SEE WITH A TELESCOPE FROM EARTH! DON'T YOU REMEMBER ANYTHING FROM YOUR BRIEFINGS ABOUT THE JOURNEY?
DON'T BE SILLY! ONE OF THOSE ASTROLOGISTS EVEN CLAIMED THAT THE MARTIANS WERE MORE ADVANCED THAN US HUMANS!
ASTRONOMERS! AND WHY SHOULD YOU BE SURPRISED? IMAGINE THE TECHNOLOGY NECESSARY TO CONSTRUCT A CANAL SYSTEM THAT CAN IRRIGATE AN ENTIRE PLANET!
YOUR "CANALS" APPEAR TO BE NOTHING MORE THAN NATURAL GORGES!
IS IT REALLY SO HARD TO BELIEVE THAT THERE ARE BEINGS IN THE UNIVERSE MORE EVOLVED THAN YOU?
OF COURSE IT IS...
I'M GERMAN!
SOPHIE! THE GROUND'S GETTING REALLY CLOSE! HOW'S THE FORWARD SKID?
IT'S STILL STUCK!

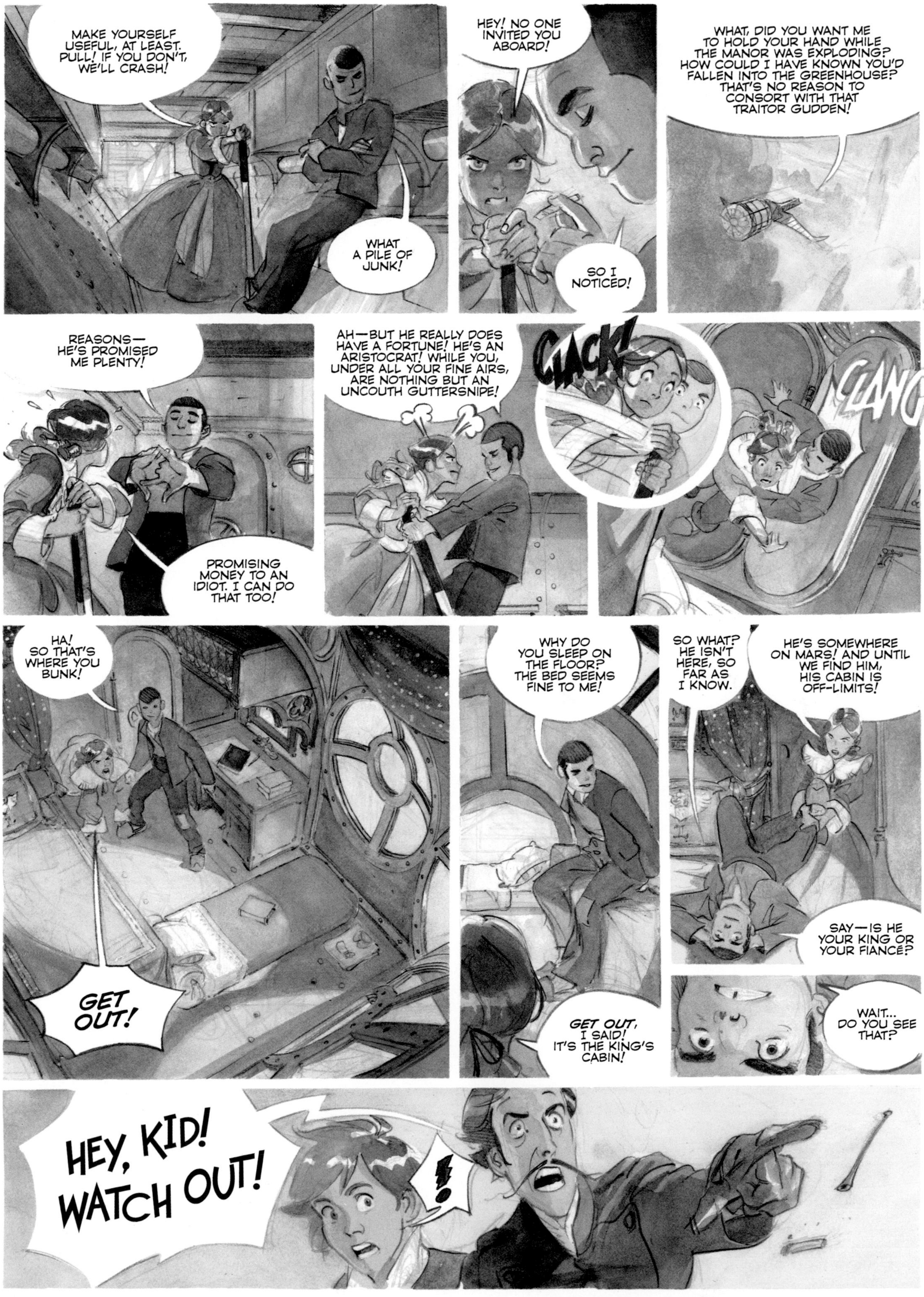
MAKE YOURSELF USEFUL, AT LEAST. PULL! IF YOU DON'T, WE'LL CRASH!
WHAT A PILE OF JUNK!
HEY! NO ONE INVITED YOU ABOARD!
SO I NOTICED!
WHAT, DID YOU WANT ME TO HOLD YOUR HAND WHILE THE MANOR WAS EXPLODING? HOW COULD I HAVE KNOWN YOU'D FALLEN INTO THE GREENHOUSE? THAT'S NO REASON TO CONSORT WITH THAT TRAITOR GUDDEN!
REASONS—HE'S PROMISED ME PLENTY!
PROMISING MONEY TO AN IDIOT. I CAN DO THAT TOO!
AH—BUT HE REALLY DOES HAVE A FORTUNE! HE'S AN ARISTOCRAT! WHILE YOU, UNDER ALL YOUR FINE AIRS, ARE NOTHING BUT AN UNCOUTH GUTTERSNIPE!
CLACK!
CLANG
HA! SO THAT'S WHERE YOU BUNK!
GET OUT!
WHY DO YOU SLEEP ON THE FLOOR? THE BED SEEMS FINE TO ME!
GET OUT, I SAID! IT'S THE KING'S CABIN!
SO WHAT? HE ISN'T HERE, SO FAR AS I KNOW.
HE'S SOMEWHERE ON MARS! AND UNTIL WE FIND HIM, HIS CABIN IS OFF-LIMITS!
SAY—IS HE YOUR KING OR YOUR FIANCÉ?
WAIT... DO YOU SEE THAT?
HEY, KID! WATCH OUT!
!

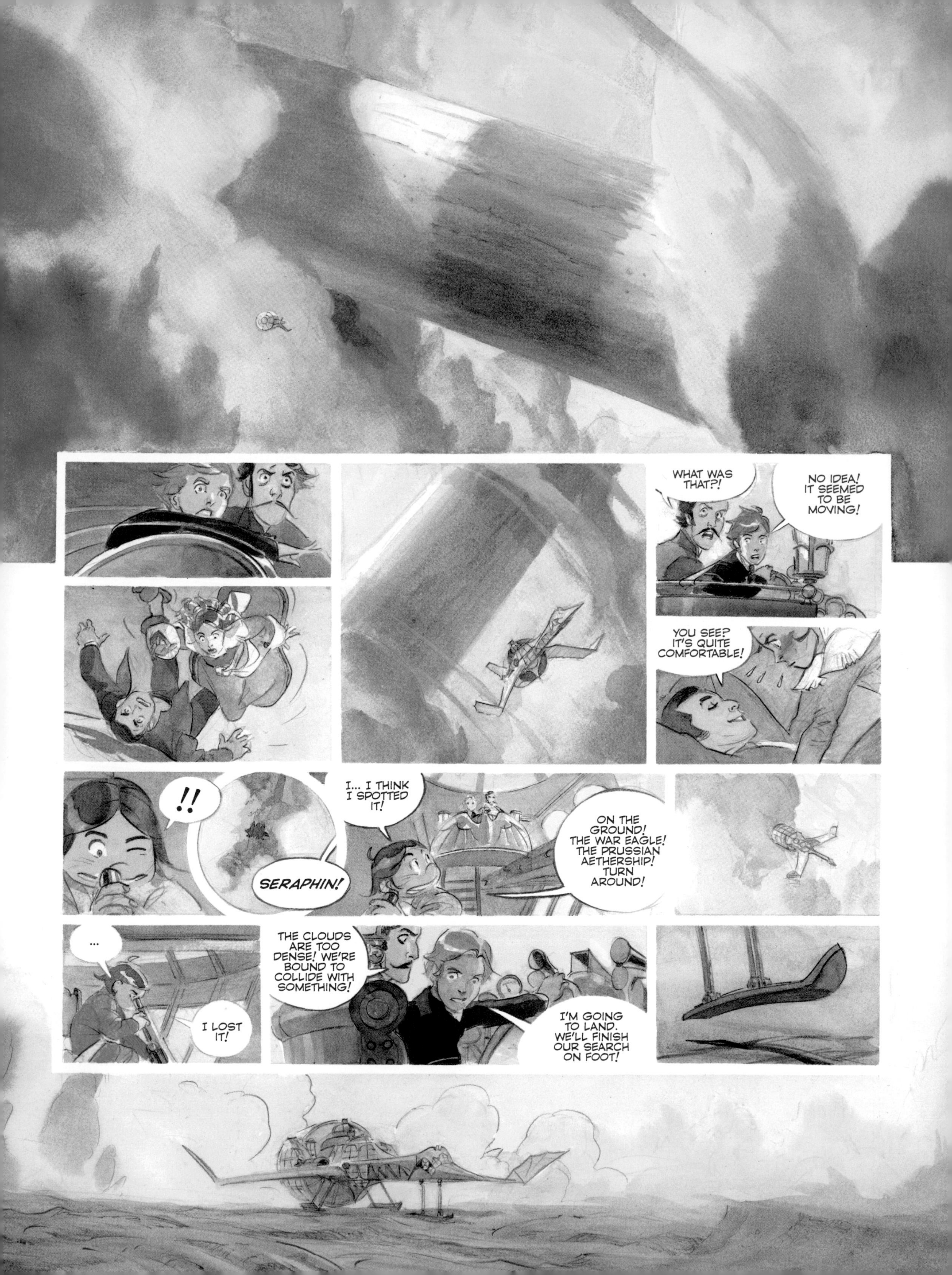
WHAT WAS THAT?!
NO IDEA! IT SEEMED TO BE MOVING!
YOU SEE? IT'S QUITE COMFORTABLE!
!!
SERAPHIN!
I... I THINK I SPOTTED IT!
ON THE GROUND! THE WAR EAGLE! THE PRUSSIAN AETHERSHIP! TURN AROUND!
...
I LOST IT!
THE CLOUDS ARE TOO DENSE! WE'RE BOUND TO COLLIDE WITH SOMETHING!
I'M GOING TO LAND. WE'LL FINISH OUR SEARCH ON FOOT!

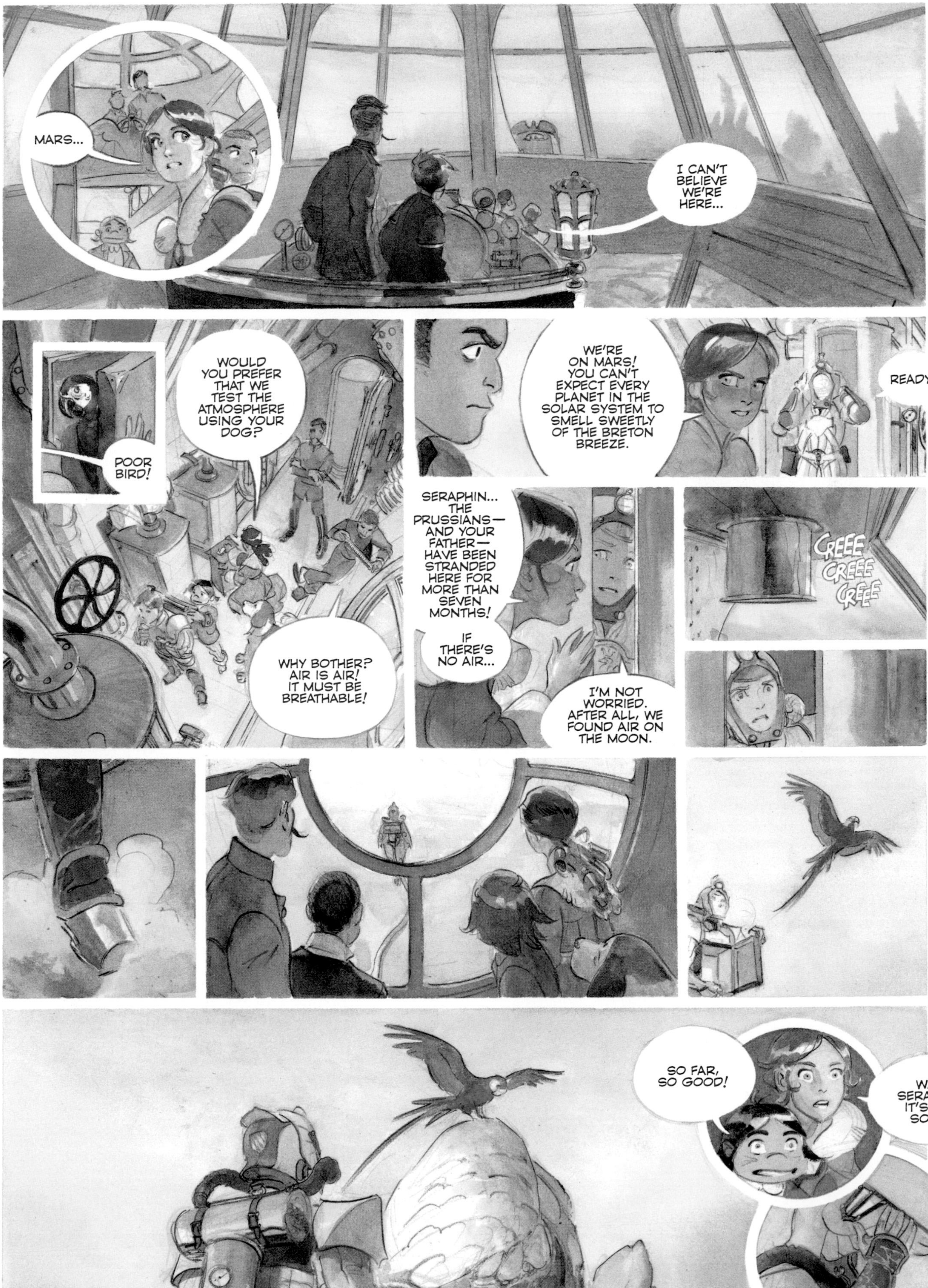
MARS...
I CAN'T BELIEVE WE'RE HERE...
WOULD YOU PREFER THAT WE TEST THE ATMOSPHERE USING YOUR DOG?
POOR BIRD!
WHY BOTHER? AIR IS AIR! IT MUST BE BREATHABLE!
WE'RE ON MARS! YOU CAN'T EXPECT EVERY PLANET IN THE SOLAR SYSTEM TO SMELL SWEETLY OF THE BRETON BREEZE.
READY!
SERAPHIN... THE PRUSSIANS—AND YOUR FATHER—HAVE BEEN STRANDED HERE FOR MORE THAN SEVEN MONTHS!
IF THERE'S NO AIR...
I'M NOT WORRIED. AFTER ALL, WE FOUND AIR ON THE MOON.
CREEE CREEE CREEE
SO FAR, SO GOOD!
WAIT, SERAPHIN! IT'S TOO SOON!
PSHEEEEE.

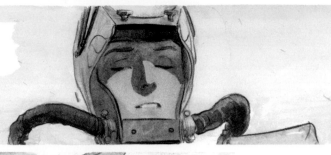

Metallic. Mineral. Dry, despite the mist... Thinner than on Earth, but also purer...

I will never forget the air of HER planet.

SO MARS IS HABITABLE! THE CREW OF THE WAR EAGLE COULD HAVE SURVIVED!

I TOLD YOU SO!

THE ROCK— IT'S MOVING!

SIGNAL HIM TO RETURN. ONCE HE'S BACK, I'LL TAKE CHARGE OF THE EXPEDITION...

...

WHAT'S HE DOING?

HE'S SETTING OFF ON HIS OWN!

BUT...

SERAPHIN!!

HEY!

GET BACK HERE!

!

STOP! I'M IN COMMAND OF THIS EXPEDITION! PREPARE MY SPACE SUIT AND WEAPONS! YOU WILL REMAIN ON BOARD!

BUT...

YOU WILL OBEY MY ORDERS! SOMEONE MUST KEEP THIS GNOME FROM STEALING THE SHIP!

YOU'VE GOT TO BE KIDDING! EVEN IF I COULD FLY THIS CRAFT, I WOULDN'T LEAVE WITHOUT MY SISTER AND MY BUDDY!

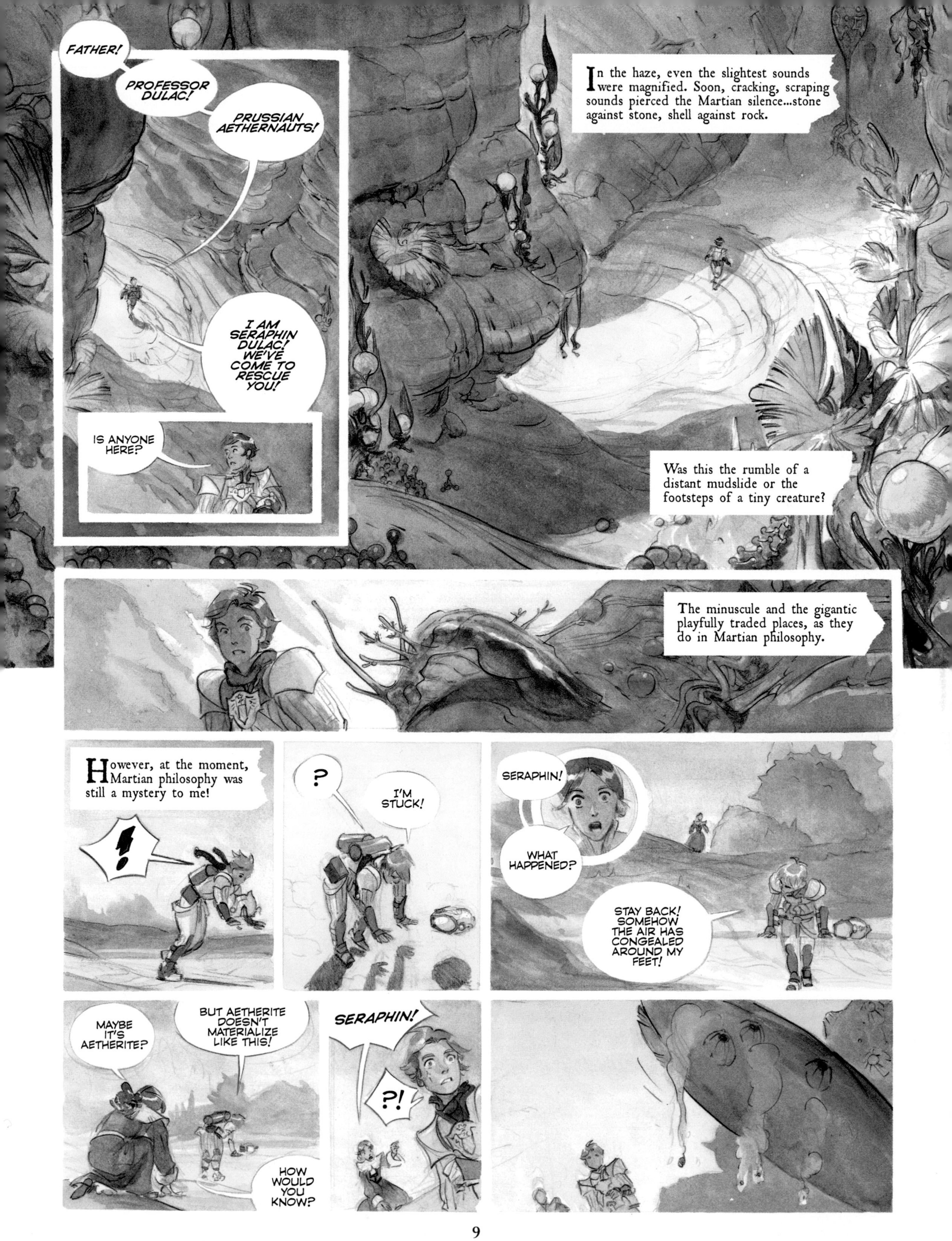

FATHER!
PROFESSOR DULAC!
PRUSSIAN AETHERNAUTS!
In the haze, even the slightest sounds were magnified. Soon, cracking, scraping sounds pierced the Martian silence...stone against stone, shell against rock.
I AM SERAPHIN DULAC! WE'VE COME TO RESCUE YOU!
IS ANYONE HERE?
Was this the rumble of a distant mudslide or the footsteps of a tiny creature?
The minuscule and the gigantic playfully traded places, as they do in Martian philosophy.
However, at the moment, Martian philosophy was still a mystery to me!
!
?
I'M STUCK!
SERAPHIN!
WHAT HAPPENED?
STAY BACK! SOMEHOW THE AIR HAS CONGEALED AROUND MY FEET!
MAYBE IT'S AETHERITE?
BUT AETHERITE DOESN'T MATERIALIZE LIKE THIS!
HOW WOULD YOU KNOW?
SERAPHIN!
?!

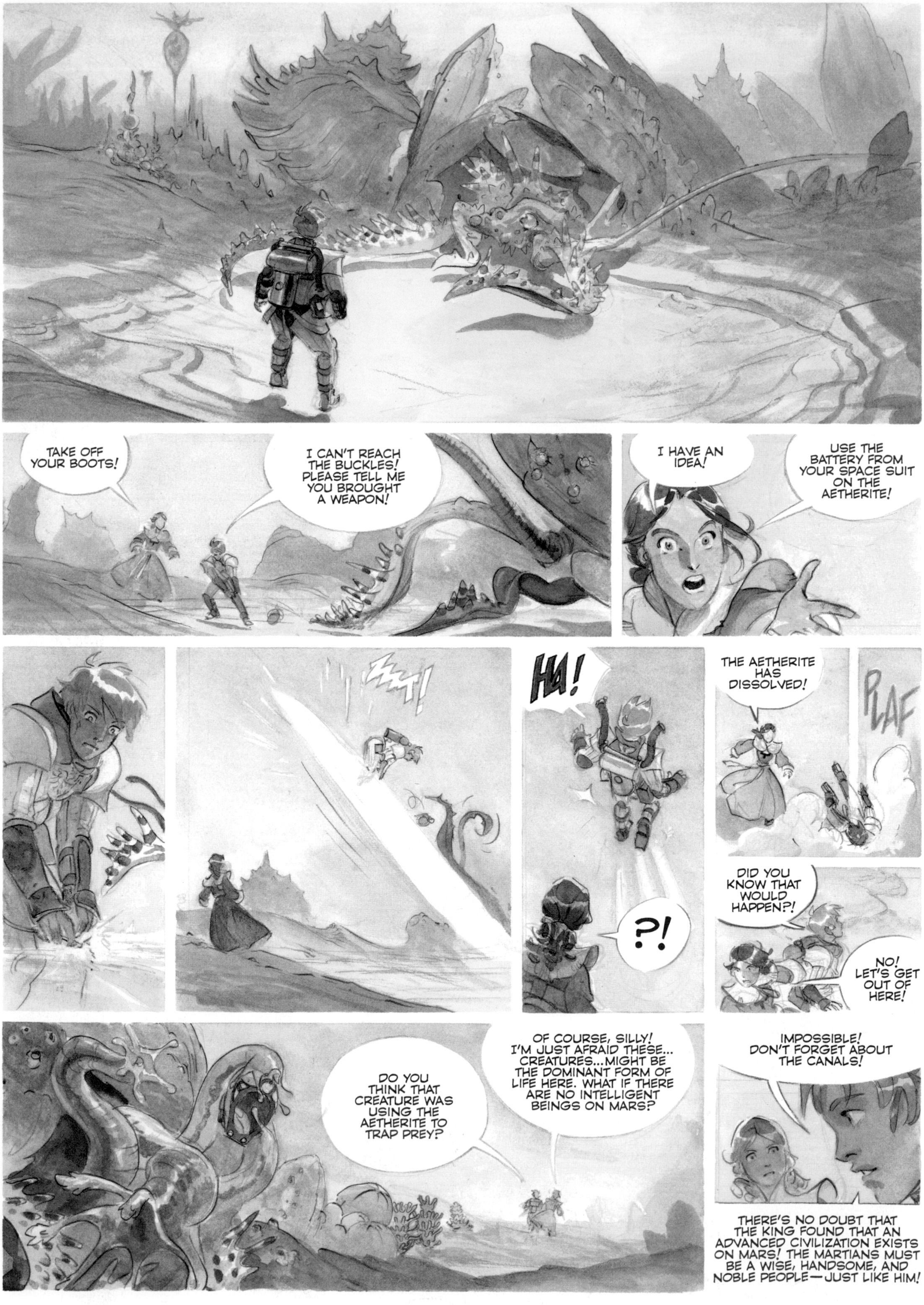
TAKE OFF YOUR BOOTS!
I CAN'T REACH THE BUCKLES! PLEASE TELL ME YOU BROUGHT A WEAPON!
I HAVE AN IDEA!
USE THE BATTERY FROM YOUR SPACE SUIT ON THE AETHERITE!
ZZT!
HA!
?!
THE AETHERITE HAS DISSOLVED!
PLAF
DID YOU KNOW THAT WOULD HAPPEN?!
NO! LET'S GET OUT OF HERE!
DO YOU THINK THAT CREATURE WAS USING THE AETHERITE TO TRAP PREY?
OF COURSE, SILLY! I'M JUST AFRAID THESE... CREATURES...MIGHT BE THE DOMINANT FORM OF LIFE HERE. WHAT IF THERE ARE NO INTELLIGENT BEINGS ON MARS?
IMPOSSIBLE! DON'T FORGET ABOUT THE CANALS!
THERE'S NO DOUBT THAT THE KING FOUND THAT AN ADVANCED CIVILIZATION EXISTS ON MARS! THE MARTIANS MUST BE A WISE, HANDSOME, AND NOBLE PEOPLE—JUST LIKE HIM!

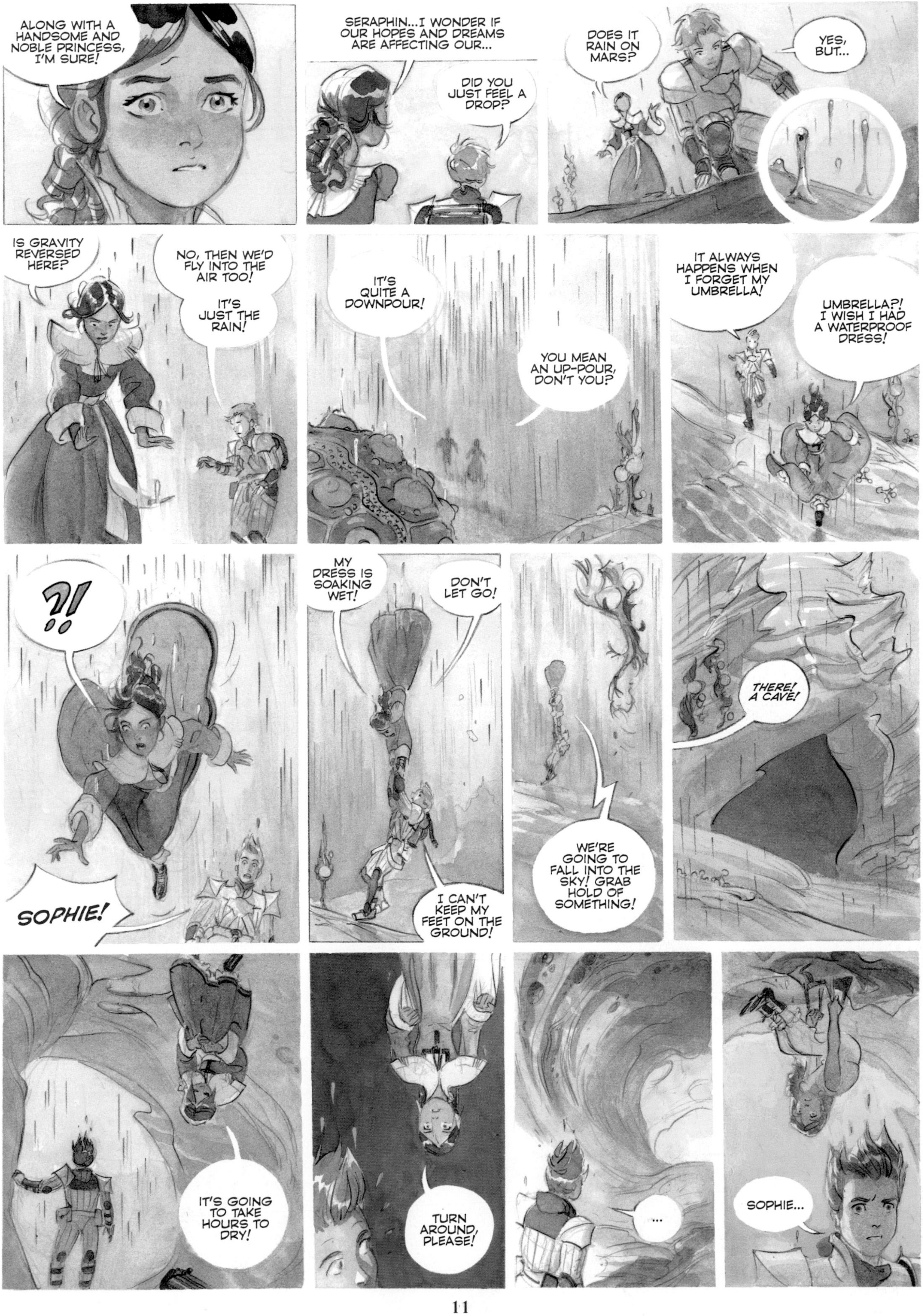
ALONG WITH A HANDSOME AND NOBLE PRINCESS, I'M SURE!
SERAPHIN...I WONDER IF OUR HOPES AND DREAMS ARE AFFECTING OUR...
DID YOU JUST FEEL A DROP?
DOES IT RAIN ON MARS?
YES, BUT...
IS GRAVITY REVERSED HERE?
NO, THEN WE'D FLY INTO THE AIR TOO!
IT'S JUST THE RAIN!
IT'S QUITE A DOWNPOUR!
YOU MEAN AN UP-POUR, DON'T YOU?
IT ALWAYS HAPPENS WHEN I FORGET MY UMBRELLA!
UMBRELLA?! I WISH I HAD A WATERPROOF DRESS!
?!
SOPHIE!
MY DRESS IS SOAKING WET!
DON'T LET GO!
I CAN'T KEEP MY FEET ON THE GROUND!
WE'RE GOING TO FALL INTO THE SKY! GRAB HOLD OF SOMETHING!
THERE! A CAVE!
IT'S GOING TO TAKE HOURS TO DRY!
TURN AROUND, PLEASE!
...
SOPHIE...

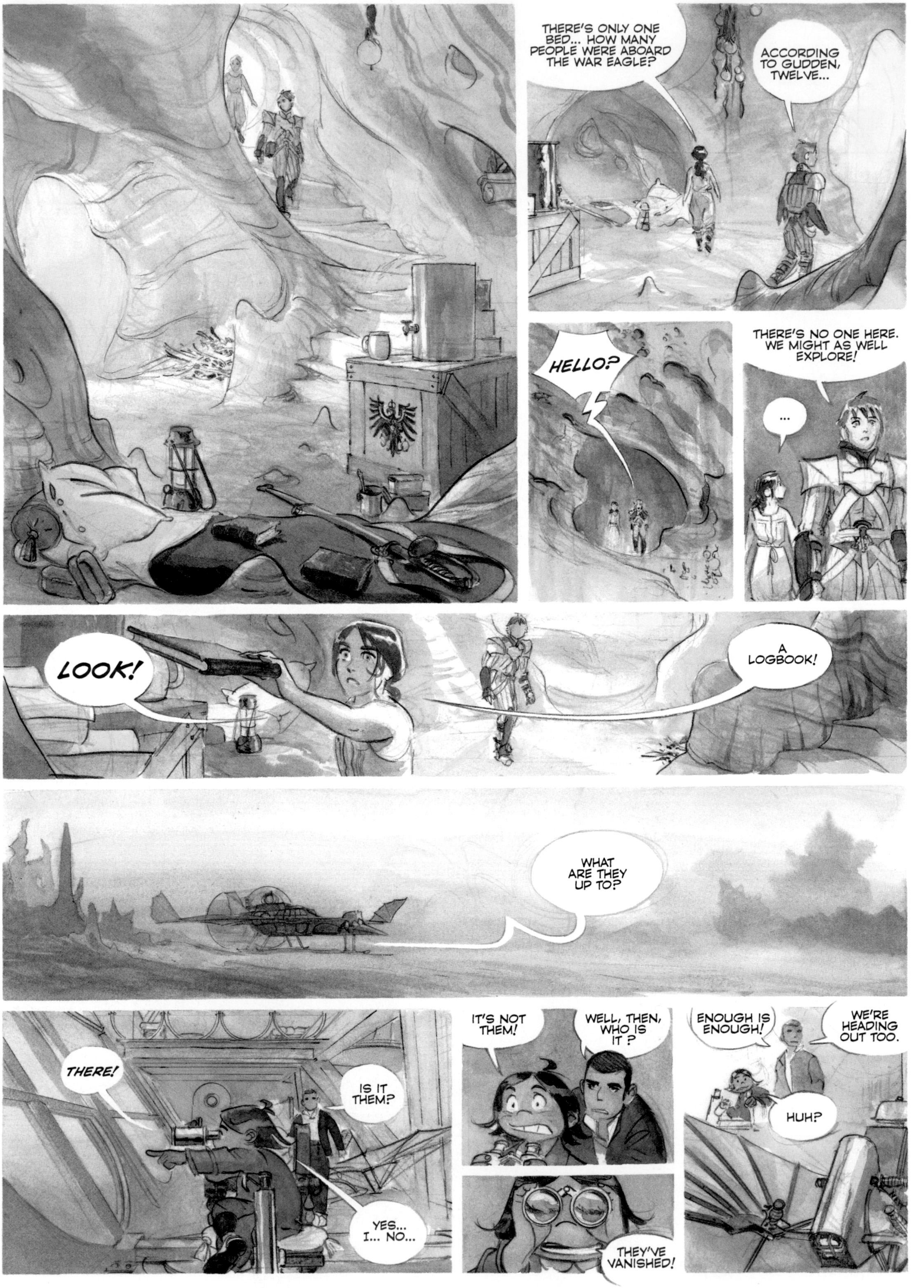
THERE'S ONLY ONE BED... HOW MANY PEOPLE WERE ABOARD THE WAR EAGLE?
ACCORDING TO GUDDEN, TWELVE...
HELLO?
THERE'S NO ONE HERE. WE MIGHT AS WELL EXPLORE!
...
LOOK!
A LOGBOOK!
WHAT ARE THEY UP TO?
THERE!
IS IT THEM?
YES... I... NO...
IT'S NOT THEM!
WELL, THEN, WHO IS IT ?
THEY'VE VANISHED!
ENOUGH IS ENOUGH!
WE'RE HEADING OUT TOO.
HUH?

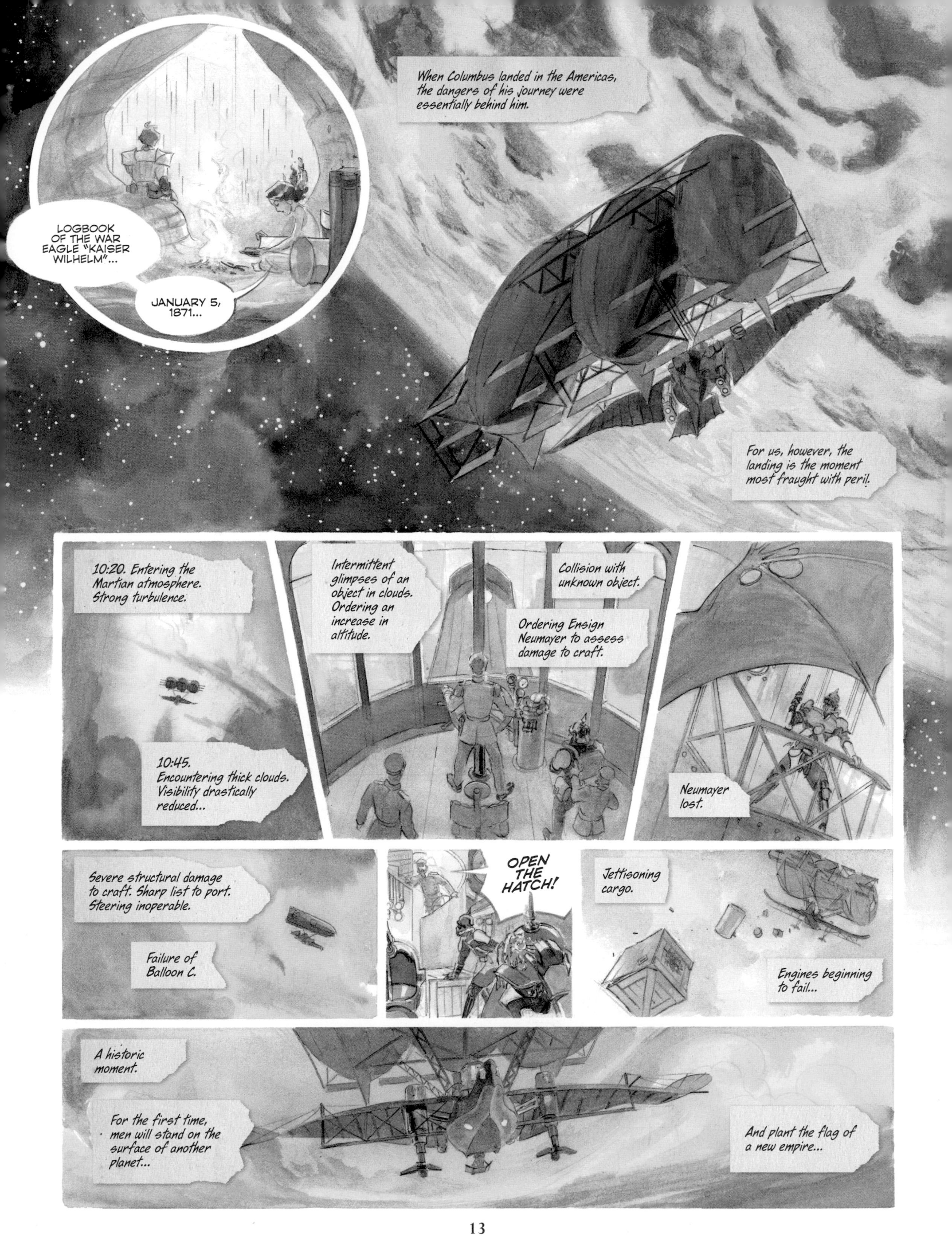
LOGBOOK OF THE WAR EAGLE "KAISER WILHELM"...
JANUARY 5, 1871...
When Columbus landed in the Americas, the dangers of his journey were essentially behind him.
For us, however, the landing is the moment most fraught with peril.
10:20. Entering the Martian atmosphere. Strong turbulence.
10:45. Encountering thick clouds. Visibility drastically reduced...
Intermittent glimpses of an object in clouds. Ordering an increase in altitude.
Collision with unknown object.
Ordering Ensign Neumayer to assess damage to craft.
Neumayer lost.
Severe structural damage to craft. Sharp list to port. Steering inoperable.
Failure of Balloon C.
OPEN THE HATCH!
Jettisoning cargo.
Engines beginning to fail...
A historic moment.
For the first time, men will stand on the surface of another planet...
And plant the flag of a new empire...

"...WITH OUR SUCCESS, ALL HUMANITY TRIUMPHS!"

ONLY ONE OF THEIR BALLOONS BURST? MY FATHER COULD HAVE REPAIRED THAT WITHOUT ANY PROBLEM!

LET ME FINISH!

PROFESSOR HAECKEL?!

"WHILE THE CRAFT WAS BEING REPAIRED, THE CAPTAIN ORGANIZED A SCIENTIFIC EXPEDITION..." HERE IT IS! "PROFESSOR HAECKEL LEFT WITH THREE MEN..."

MUST BE A CODE NAME...

OR THEY HAD TWO PROFESSORS ABOARD!

January 12... Major Kley returned to base camp alone.

He was ranting incoherently...

I am mounting a rescue operation with four men. The haze is thick, but we shall set out toward the Grand Canal.

January 15.

Dessoff and Reichenbach are dead.

No trace of the professor.

January 16.

Encountered a rock formation resembling a globe of Mars.

We have many questions, but no answers. Professor remains missing.

7:00.
On reconnaissance mission, Mueller empties his magazine into the haze...

Then hurls himself off a cliff, shouting nonsense.

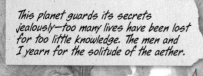

This planet guards its secrets jealously—too many lives have been lost for too little knowledge. The men and I yearn for the solitude of the aether.

I hope that repairs to the airship have been completed now that the storm is over.

I have no choice now but to abandon the professor to his fate.

KEEP READING.

14

January 17. Another death. But at last we know the cause.

We have been the victims of hallucinations!

The visions come suddenly, without any warning. An ally becomes an enemy, a comrade becomes a monstrous foe!

My own nightmarish visions nearly cost Wilbrand his life.

I regained my sanity just in time.

We must leave this place as quickly as possible.

January 18. Returned to the War Eagle...

...with our hopes in ruins.

We should never have ventured here.

THE TEXT ENDS THERE.

SERAPHIN...

THE HAZE IS LIFTING!

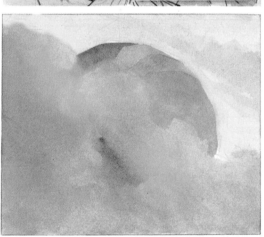

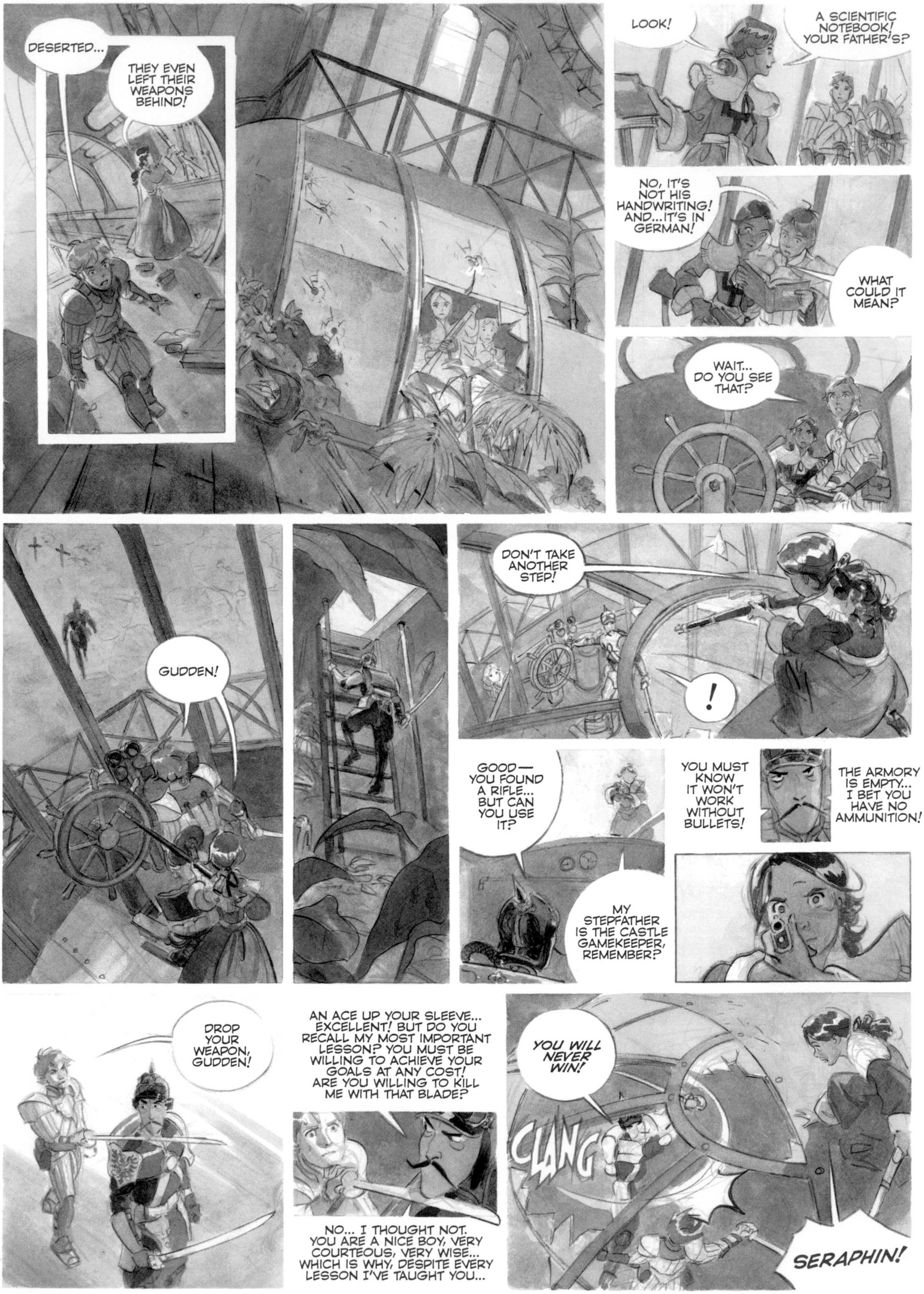
DESERTED...
THEY EVEN LEFT THEIR WEAPONS BEHIND!
LOOK!
A SCIENTIFIC NOTEBOOK! YOUR FATHER'S?
NO, IT'S NOT HIS HANDWRITING! AND...IT'S IN GERMAN!
WHAT COULD IT MEAN?
WAIT... DO YOU SEE THAT?
GUDDEN!
DON'T TAKE ANOTHER STEP!
!
GOOD— YOU FOUND A RIFLE... BUT CAN YOU USE IT?
YOU MUST KNOW IT WON'T WORK WITHOUT BULLETS!
THE ARMORY IS EMPTY... I BET YOU HAVE NO AMMUNITION!
MY STEPFATHER IS THE CASTLE GAMEKEEPER, REMEMBER?
DROP YOUR WEAPON, GUDDEN!
AN ACE UP YOUR SLEEVE... EXCELLENT! BUT DO YOU RECALL MY MOST IMPORTANT LESSON? YOU MUST BE WILLING TO ACHIEVE YOUR GOALS AT ANY COST! ARE YOU WILLING TO KILL ME WITH THAT BLADE?
NO... I THOUGHT NOT. YOU ARE A NICE BOY, VERY COURTEOUS, VERY WISE... WHICH IS WHY, DESPITE EVERY LESSON I'VE TAUGHT YOU...
YOU WILL NEVER WIN!
CLANG
SERAPHIN!

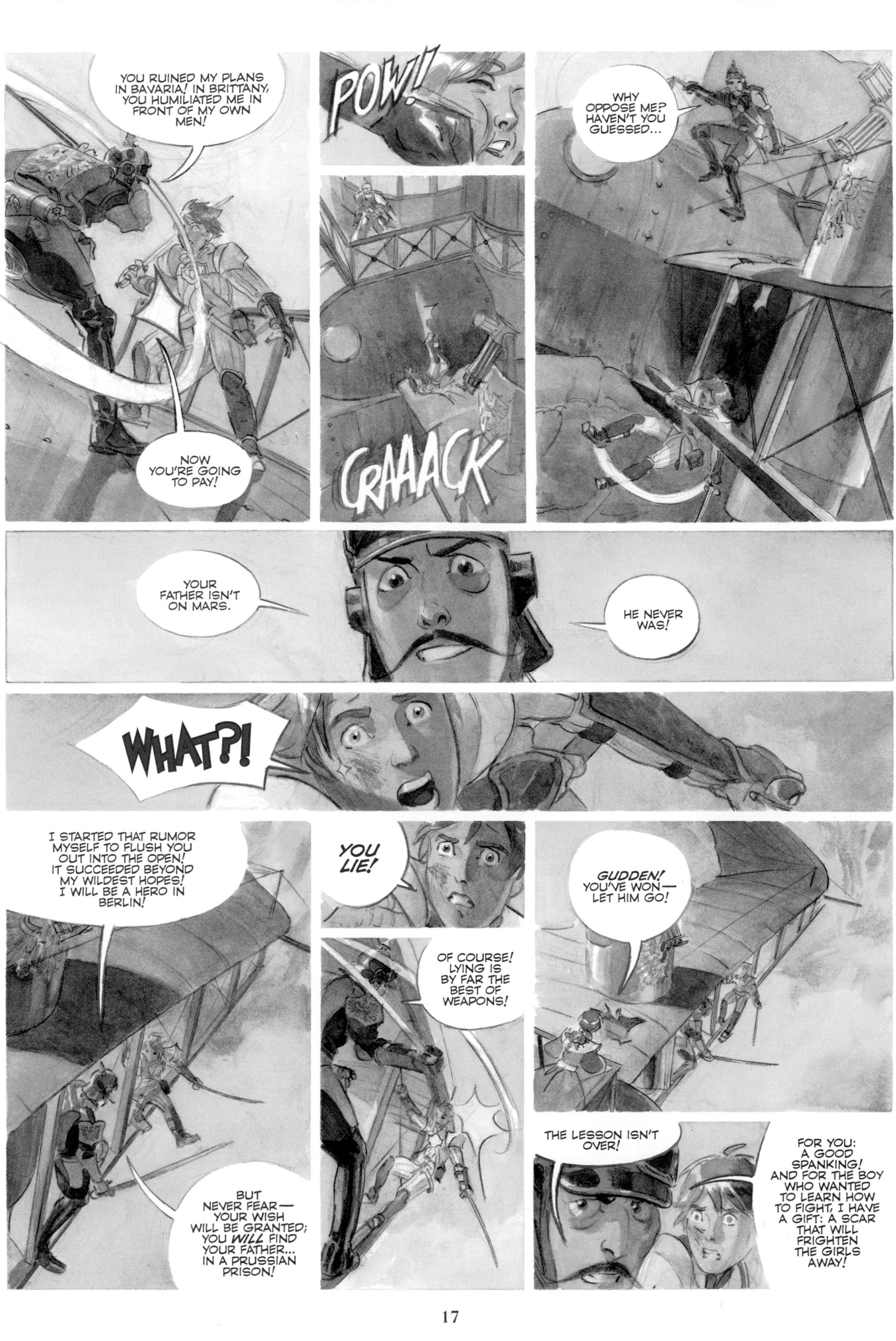
YOU RUINED MY PLANS IN BAVARIA! IN BRITTANY, YOU HUMILIATED ME IN FRONT OF MY OWN MEN!
NOW YOU'RE GOING TO PAY!
POW!!
CRAAACK
WHY OPPOSE ME? HAVEN'T YOU GUESSED...
YOUR FATHER ISN'T ON MARS.
HE NEVER WAS!
WHAT?!
I STARTED THAT RUMOR MYSELF TO FLUSH YOU OUT INTO THE OPEN! IT SUCCEEDED BEYOND MY WILDEST HOPES! I WILL BE A HERO IN BERLIN!
BUT NEVER FEAR— YOUR WISH WILL BE GRANTED; YOU *WILL* FIND YOUR FATHER... IN A PRUSSIAN PRISON!
YOU LIE!
OF COURSE! LYING IS BY FAR THE BEST OF WEAPONS!
GUDDEN! YOU'VE WON— LET HIM GO!
THE LESSON ISN'T OVER!
FOR YOU: A GOOD SPANKING! AND FOR THE BOY WHO WANTED TO LEARN HOW TO FIGHT, I HAVE A GIFT: A SCAR THAT WILL FRIGHTEN THE GIRLS AWAY!

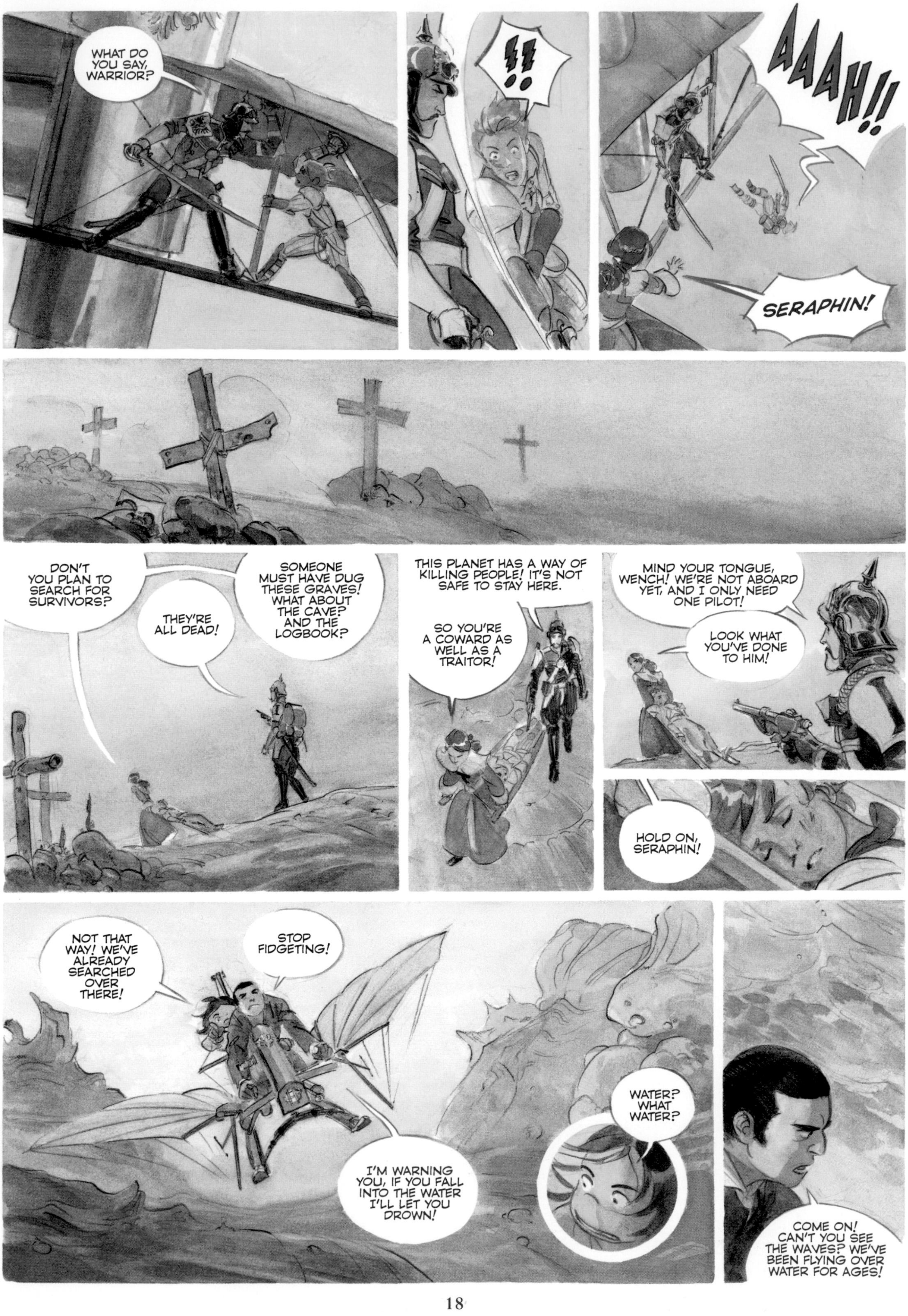
WHAT DO YOU SAY, WARRIOR?
!!
AAAH!!
SERAPHIN!
DON'T YOU PLAN TO SEARCH FOR SURVIVORS?
THEY'RE ALL DEAD!
SOMEONE MUST HAVE DUG THESE GRAVES! WHAT ABOUT THE CAVE? AND THE LOGBOOK?
THIS PLANET HAS A WAY OF KILLING PEOPLE! IT'S NOT SAFE TO STAY HERE.
SO YOU'RE A COWARD AS WELL AS A TRAITOR!
MIND YOUR TONGUE, WENCH! WE'RE NOT ABOARD YET, AND I ONLY NEED ONE PILOT!
LOOK WHAT YOU'VE DONE TO HIM!
HOLD ON, SERAPHIN!
NOT THAT WAY! WE'VE ALREADY SEARCHED OVER THERE!
STOP FIDGETING!
I'M WARNING YOU, IF YOU FALL INTO THE WATER I'LL LET YOU DROWN!
WATER? WHAT WATER?
COME ON! CAN'T YOU SEE THE WAVES? WE'VE BEEN FLYING OVER WATER FOR AGES!

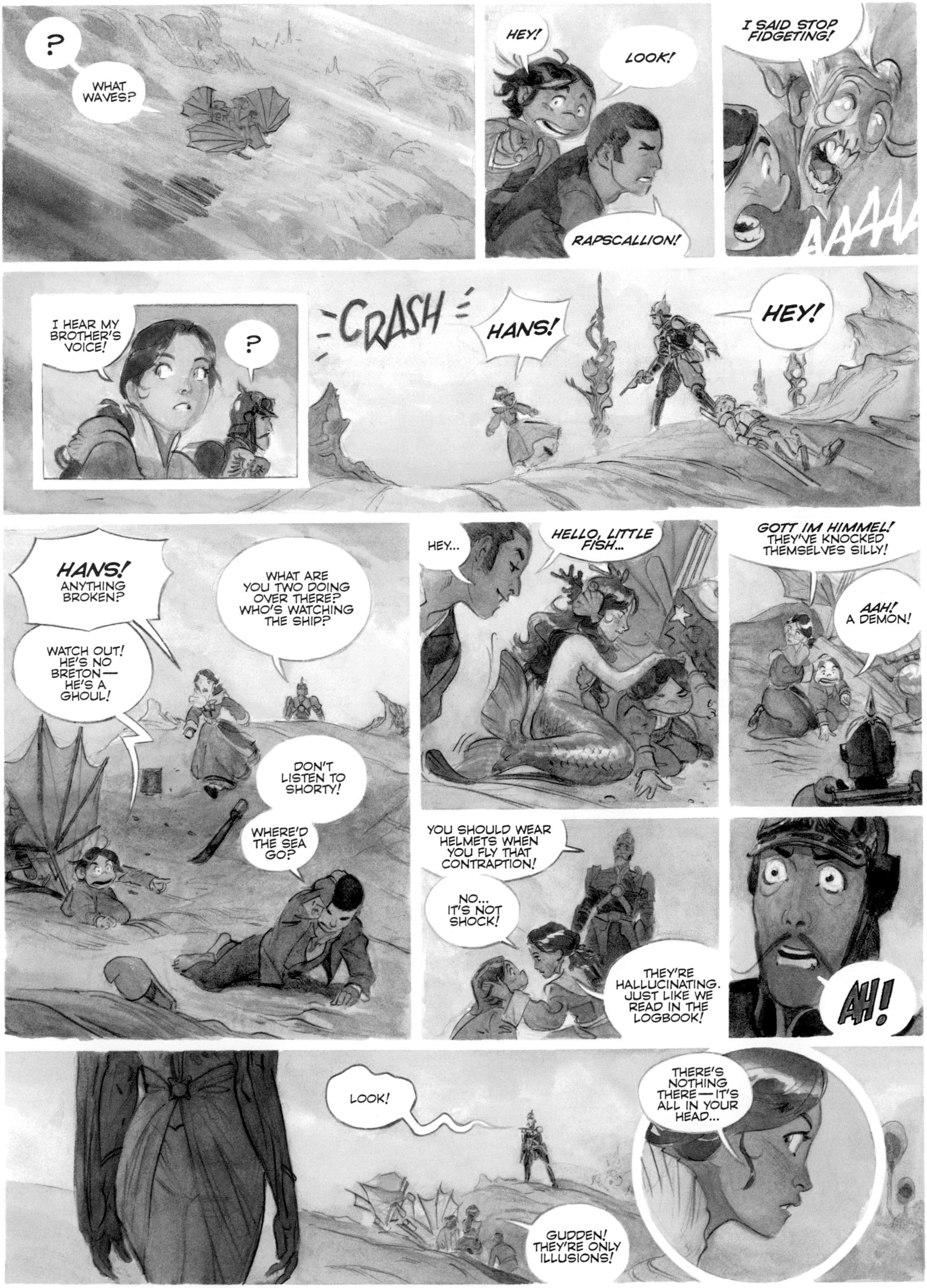
?
WHAT WAVES?
HEY!
LOOK!
RAPSCALLION!
I SAID STOP FIDGETING!
AAAAA
I HEAR MY BROTHER'S VOICE!
?
CRASH
HANS!
HEY!
HANS! ANYTHING BROKEN?
WHAT ARE YOU TWO DOING OVER THERE? WHO'S WATCHING THE SHIP?
WATCH OUT! HE'S NO BRETON—HE'S A GHOUL!
DON'T LISTEN TO SHORTY!
WHERE'D THE SEA GO?
HEY...
HELLO, LITTLE FISH...
GOTT IM HIMMEL! THEY'VE KNOCKED THEMSELVES SILLY!
AAH! A DEMON!
YOU SHOULD WEAR HELMETS WHEN YOU FLY THAT CONTRAPTION!
NO... IT'S NOT SHOCK!
THEY'RE HALLUCINATING. JUST LIKE WE READ IN THE LOGBOOK!
AH!
LOOK!
THERE'S NOTHING THERE—IT'S ALL IN YOUR HEAD...
GUDDEN! THEY'RE ONLY ILLUSIONS!

YOUR MAJESTY! IT'S YOU!
HOW DID YOU FIND US?
WE'VE TRAVELED SO FAR...
IT'S A MIRACLE!
IT'S...
IT'S...
IT'S NOT REAL.
IT'S JUST AN ILLUSION!
WHO ARE YOU?
OH.
CLICK
HALT, DEMON!
GUDDEN! NO!

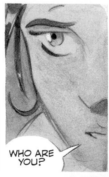

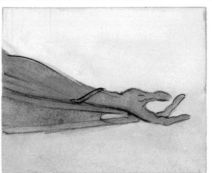

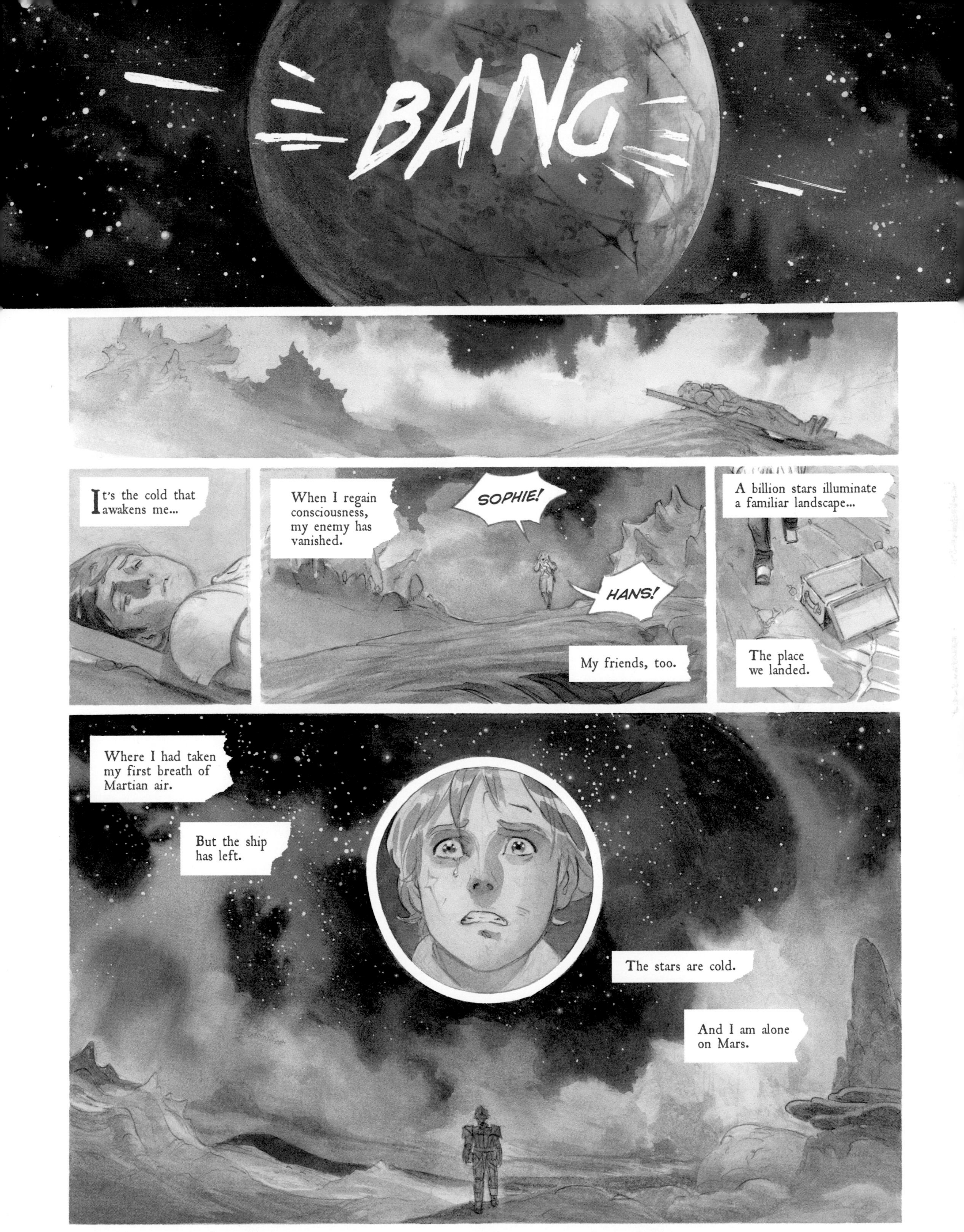
BANG
It's the cold that awakens me...
When I regain consciousness, my enemy has vanished.
SOPHIE!
HANS!
My friends, too.
A billion stars illuminate a familiar landscape...
The place we landed.
Where I had taken my first breath of Martian air.
But the ship has left.
The stars are cold.
And I am alone on Mars.

CHAPTER 11

THE PRINCESS EVANESCENT

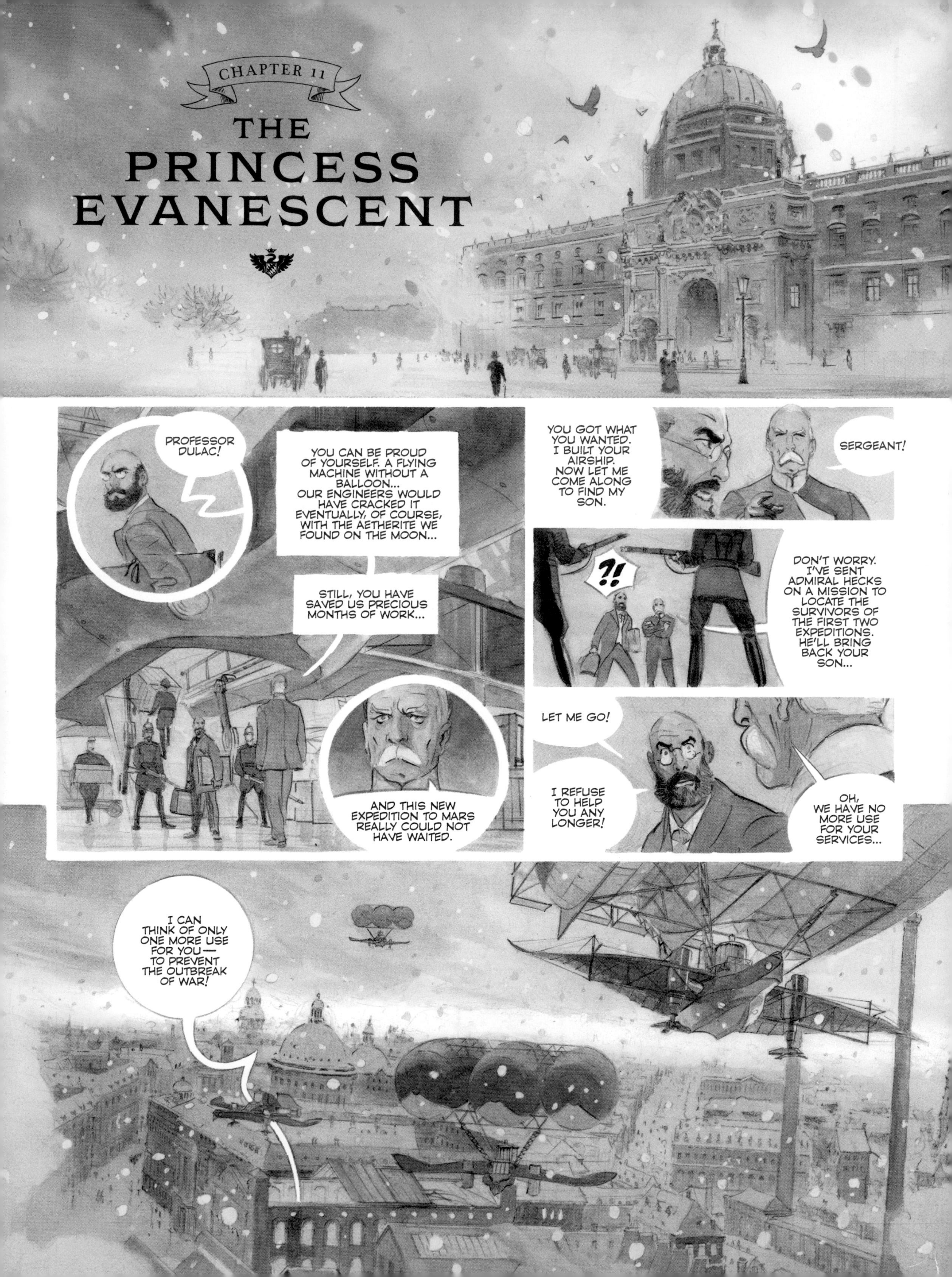
PROFESSOR DULAC!
YOU CAN BE PROUD OF YOURSELF. A FLYING MACHINE WITHOUT A BALLOON... OUR ENGINEERS WOULD HAVE CRACKED IT EVENTUALLY, OF COURSE, WITH THE AETHERITE WE FOUND ON THE MOON...
STILL, YOU HAVE SAVED US PRECIOUS MONTHS OF WORK...
AND THIS NEW EXPEDITION TO MARS REALLY COULD NOT HAVE WAITED.
YOU GOT WHAT YOU WANTED. I BUILT YOUR AIRSHIP. NOW LET ME COME ALONG TO FIND MY SON.
SERGEANT!
?!
DON'T WORRY. I'VE SENT ADMIRAL HECKS ON A MISSION TO LOCATE THE SURVIVORS OF THE FIRST TWO EXPEDITIONS. HE'LL BRING BACK YOUR SON...
LET ME GO!
I REFUSE TO HELP YOU ANY LONGER!
OH, WE HAVE NO MORE USE FOR YOUR SERVICES...
I CAN THINK OF ONLY ONE MORE USE FOR YOU— TO PREVENT THE OUTBREAK OF WAR!

When you first awaken in a new place, it sometimes takes a moment to remember where you are.

This morning, I think I am still in Brittany. I feel cold— I must have fallen asleep on the beach again...

Undoubtedly, a good batch of pancakes is waiting for me at Grandfather's house.

Then, like a fist of ice, the truth strikes me in the gut.

My only consolation is knowing that my friends are safely in the aethership, heading back to Earth.

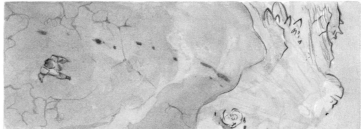

But...

!

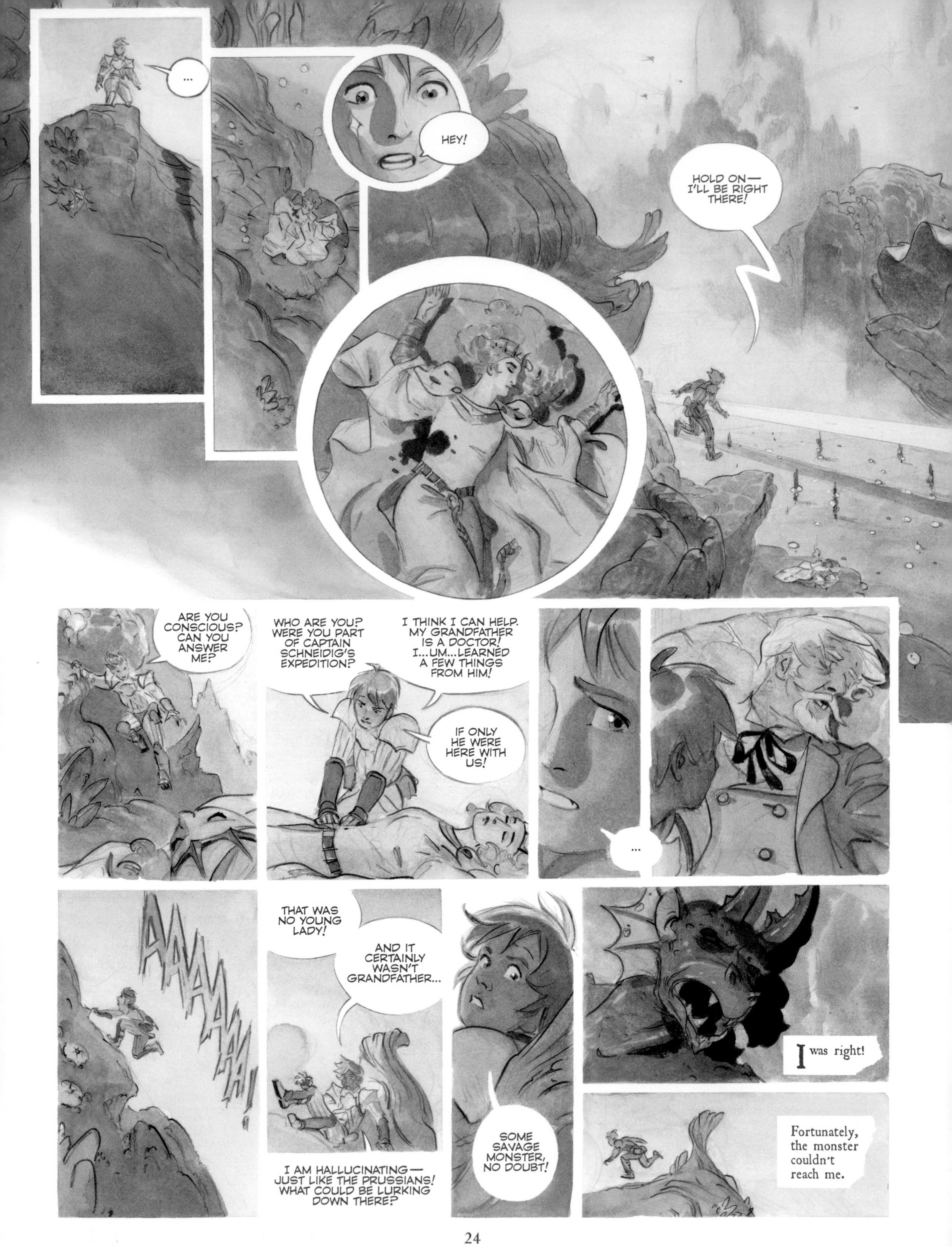
...
HEY!
HOLD ON— I'LL BE RIGHT THERE!
ARE YOU CONSCIOUS? CAN YOU ANSWER ME?
WHO ARE YOU? WERE YOU PART OF CAPTAIN SCHNEIDIG'S EXPEDITION?
I THINK I CAN HELP. MY GRANDFATHER IS A DOCTOR! I...UM...LEARNED A FEW THINGS FROM HIM!
IF ONLY HE WERE HERE WITH US!
...
AAAAAAAAA!!
THAT WAS NO YOUNG LADY!
AND IT CERTAINLY WASN'T GRANDFATHER...
I AM HALLUCINATING— JUST LIKE THE PRUSSIANS! WHAT COULD BE LURKING DOWN THERE?
SOME SAVAGE MONSTER, NO DOUBT!
I was right!
Fortunately, the monster couldn't reach me.

For me, the adventure was over. I had only to barricade myself in the cave and wait for rescue.

But who would rescue me?

No doubt the Prussians would mount a new expedition.

My only hope was to survive until they arrived and took me back to Berlin. With luck, I would join my friends and family in a Prussian prison. I had no doubt that—this time—Gudden had been telling the truth. My father had never left Earth. It was a comfort to know he was relatively safe. I, on the other hand...

Like the empress and the Austrian secret service, I had swallowed an enemy's lies. I had dragged my friends into a dangerous adventure. Whatever my punishment might be, I dreamed that an adult—any adult—would come to tell me what to do.

For the moment, I was bothered most by the thing lying on the rocks.

I hoped the creature had not survived its wounds...

She still lived...

...But would likely die soon.

Curiously, the thought of her death did not make me feel better.

As monstrous as she was, she was defenseless...

BANG   BANG   BANG

OUCH!

THERE'S NOTHING MORE I CAN DO.

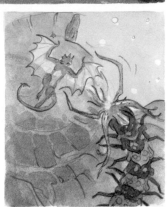

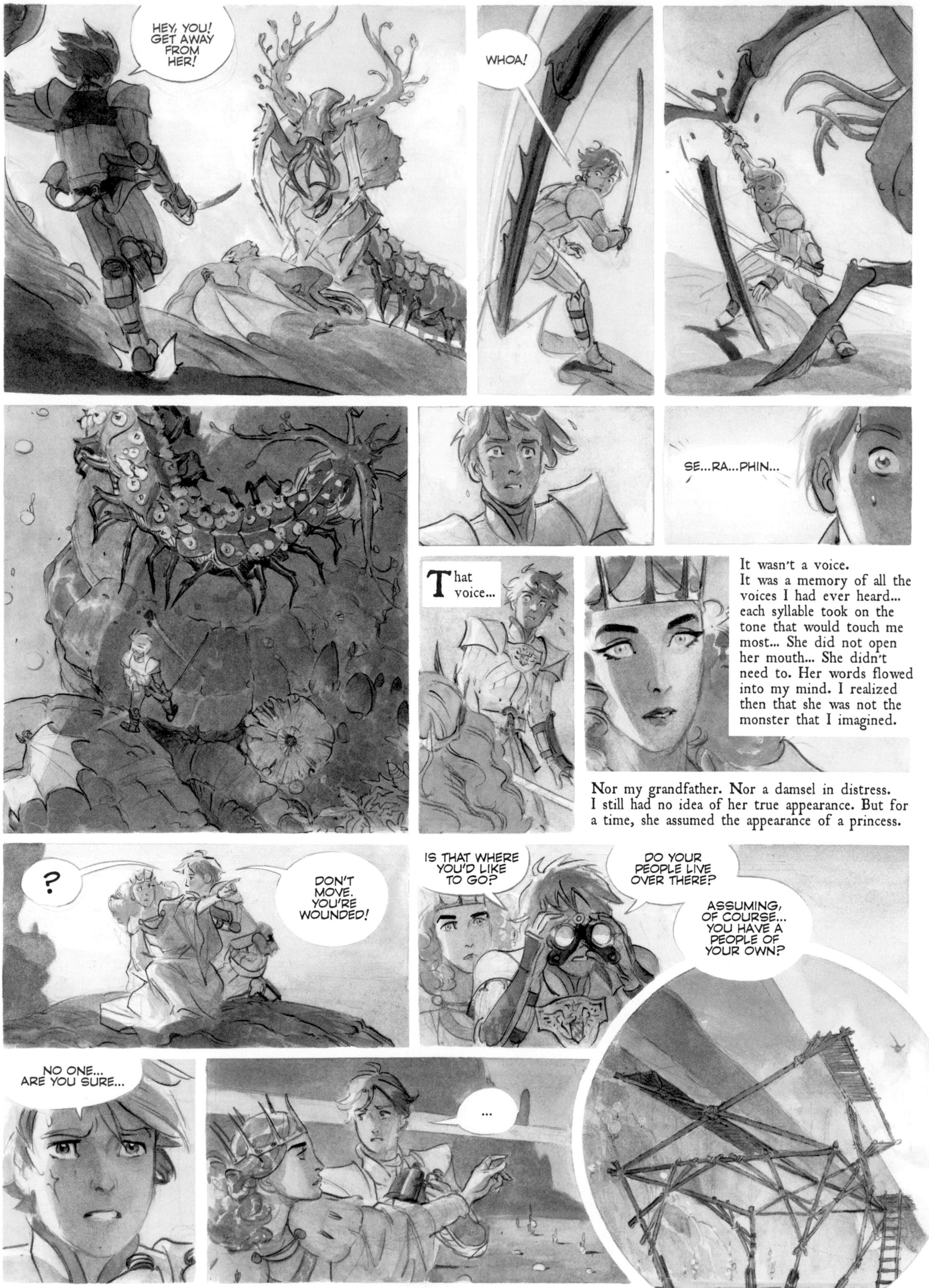
HEY, YOU! GET AWAY FROM HER!
WHOA!
SE...RA...PHIN...
That voice...
It wasn't a voice. It was a memory of all the voices I had ever heard... each syllable took on the tone that would touch me most... She did not open her mouth... She didn't need to. Her words flowed into my mind. I realized then that she was not the monster that I imagined.
Nor my grandfather. Nor a damsel in distress. I still had no idea of her true appearance. But for a time, she assumed the appearance of a princess.
?
DON'T MOVE. YOU'RE WOUNDED!
IS THAT WHERE YOU'D LIKE TO GO?
DO YOUR PEOPLE LIVE OVER THERE?
ASSUMING, OF COURSE... YOU HAVE A PEOPLE OF YOUR OWN?
NO ONE... ARE YOU SURE...
...

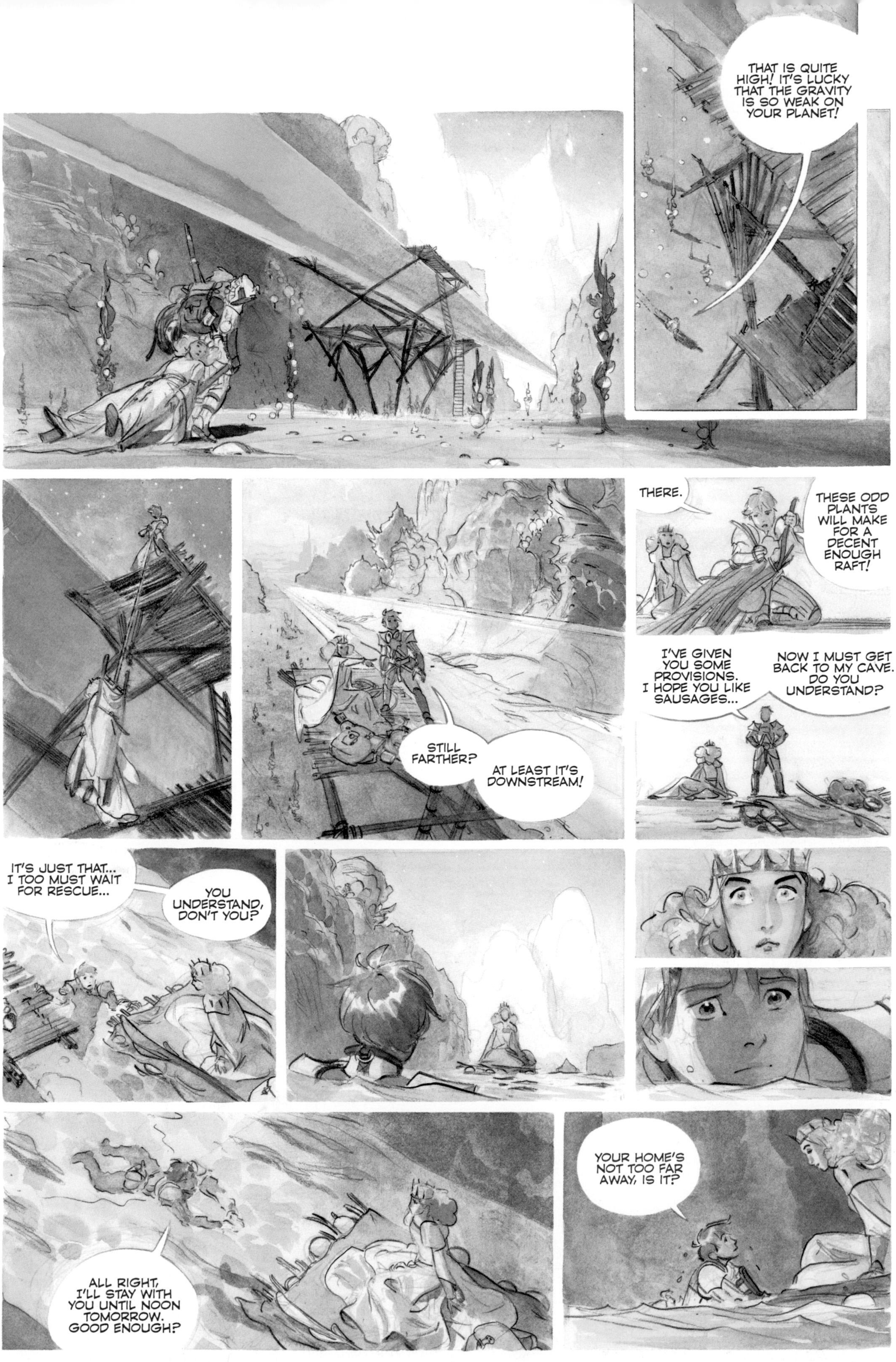
THAT IS QUITE HIGH! IT'S LUCKY THAT THE GRAVITY IS SO WEAK ON YOUR PLANET!
STILL FARTHER?
AT LEAST IT'S DOWNSTREAM!
THERE.
THESE ODD PLANTS WILL MAKE FOR A DECENT ENOUGH RAFT!
I'VE GIVEN YOU SOME PROVISIONS. I HOPE YOU LIKE SAUSAGES...
NOW I MUST GET BACK TO MY CAVE. DO YOU UNDERSTAND?
IT'S JUST THAT... I TOO MUST WAIT FOR RESCUE...
YOU UNDERSTAND, DON'T YOU?
ALL RIGHT, I'LL STAY WITH YOU UNTIL NOON TOMORROW. GOOD ENOUGH?
YOUR HOME'S NOT TOO FAR AWAY, IS IT?

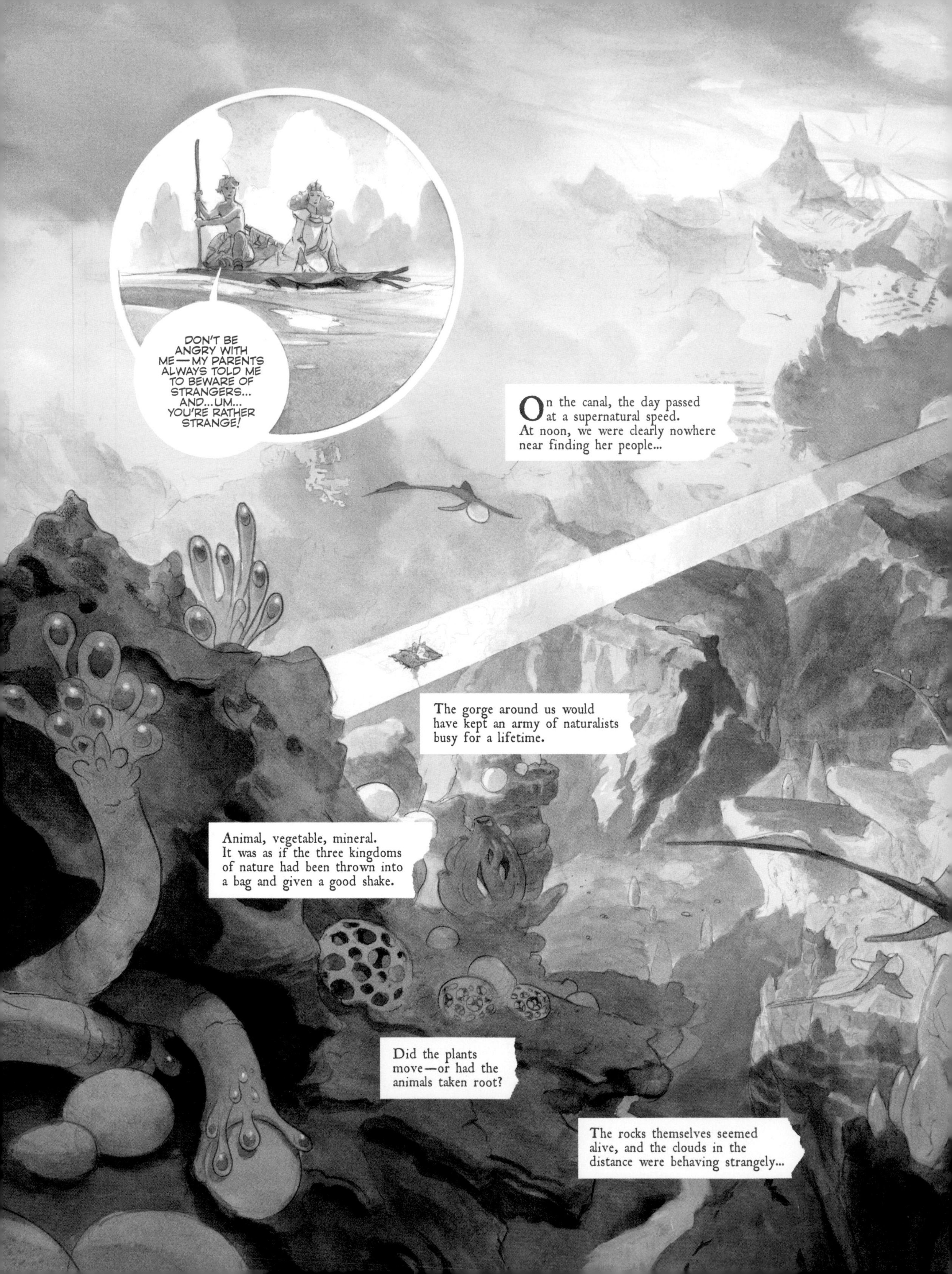
DON'T BE ANGRY WITH ME—MY PARENTS ALWAYS TOLD ME TO BEWARE OF STRANGERS... AND...UM... YOU'RE RATHER STRANGE!
On the canal, the day passed at a supernatural speed. At noon, we were clearly nowhere near finding her people...
The gorge around us would have kept an army of naturalists busy for a lifetime.
Animal, vegetable, mineral. It was as if the three kingdoms of nature had been thrown into a bag and given a good shake.
Did the plants move—or had the animals taken root?
The rocks themselves seemed alive, and the clouds in the distance were behaving strangely...

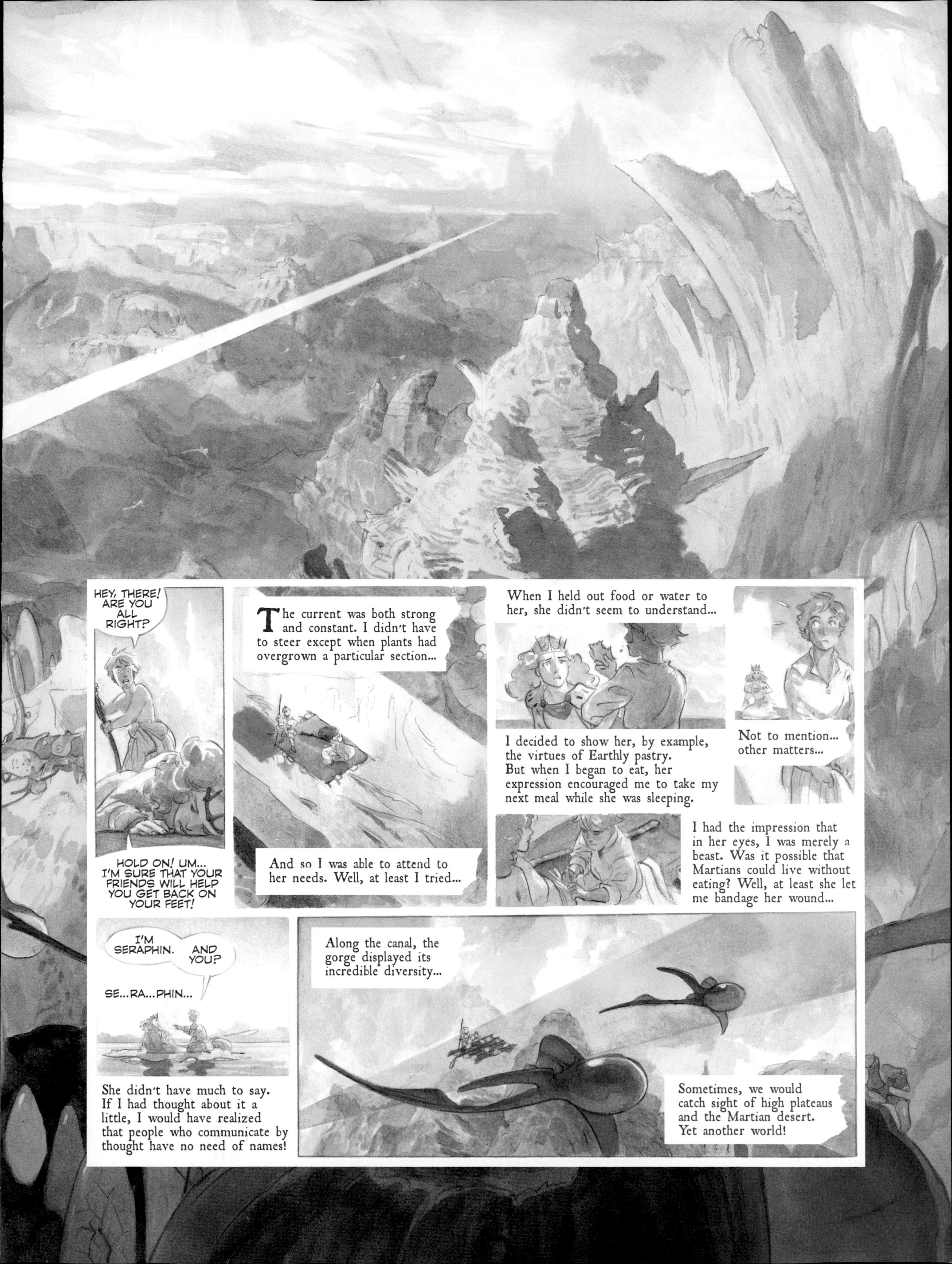
HEY, THERE! ARE YOU ALL RIGHT?
HOLD ON! UM... I'M SURE THAT YOUR FRIENDS WILL HELP YOU GET BACK ON YOUR FEET!
The current was both strong and constant. I didn't have to steer except when plants had overgrown a particular section...
And so I was able to attend to her needs. Well, at least I tried...
When I held out food or water to her, she didn't seem to understand...
I decided to show her, by example, the virtues of Earthly pastry. But when I began to eat, her expression encouraged me to take my next meal while she was sleeping.
Not to mention... other matters...
I had the impression that in her eyes, I was merely a beast. Was it possible that Martians could live without eating? Well, at least she let me bandage her wound...
I'M SERAPHIN.
AND YOU?
SE...RA...PHIN...
She didn't have much to say. If I had thought about it a little, I would have realized that people who communicate by thought have no need of names!
Along the canal, the gorge displayed its incredible diversity...
Sometimes, we would catch sight of high plateaus and the Martian desert. Yet another world!

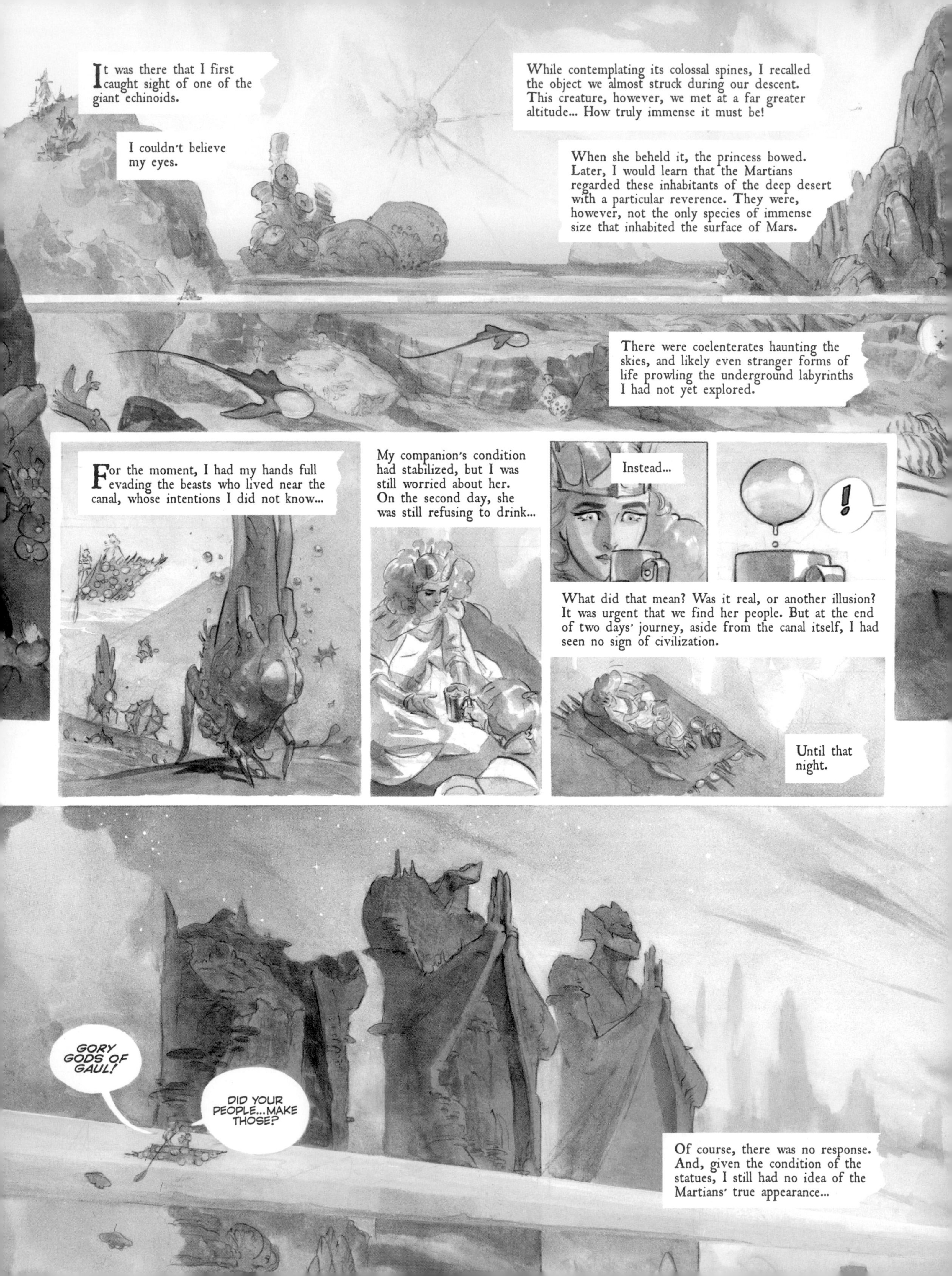

It was there that I first caught sight of one of the giant echinoids.
I couldn't believe my eyes.
While contemplating its colossal spines, I recalled the object we almost struck during our descent. This creature, however, we met at a far greater altitude... How truly immense it must be!
When she beheld it, the princess bowed. Later, I would learn that the Martians regarded these inhabitants of the deep desert with a particular reverence. They were, however, not the only species of immense size that inhabited the surface of Mars.
There were coelenterates haunting the skies, and likely even stranger forms of life prowling the underground labyrinths I had not yet explored.
For the moment, I had my hands full evading the beasts who lived near the canal, whose intentions I did not know...
My companion's condition had stabilized, but I was still worried about her. On the second day, she was still refusing to drink...
Instead...
!
What did that mean? Was it real, or another illusion? It was urgent that we find her people. But at the end of two days' journey, aside from the canal itself, I had seen no sign of civilization.
Until that night.
GORY GODS OF GAUL!
DID YOUR PEOPLE...MAKE THOSE?
Of course, there was no response. And, given the condition of the statues, I still had no idea of the Martians' true appearance...

Every night, low on the horizon, a tiny blue speck shone without twinkling...

It was a planet, and I knew that it was my home.

EARTH...

THAT'S WHERE I COME FROM!

DO YOU UNDERSTAND?

MY PLANET!

It was no use.

Did she even know what a planet was?

Earth... Where my friends were headed. Where I had left my only remaining family. My grandfather. My father.

When my father learned of all my mistakes, and the mess I'd created for myself, would he be disappointed in me? For that matter, would I ever see him again?

Or was I condemned to live out the rest of my days on this planet, in the company of strange beings whom I did not understand...

...and who would never understand me?

!

I...DO...

UNDERSTAND!

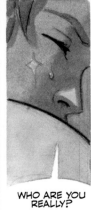
WHO ARE YOU REALLY?

31

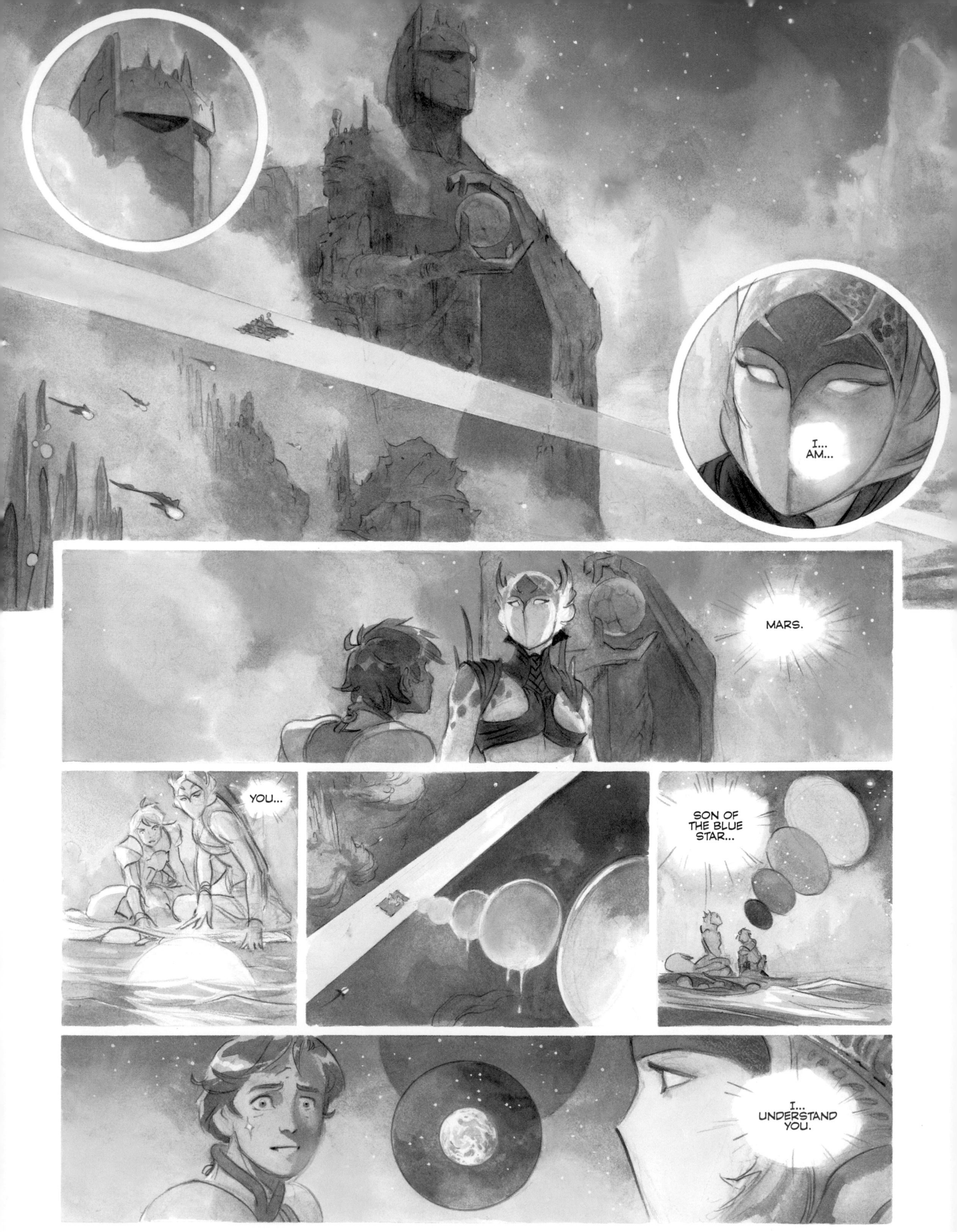
I... AM...
MARS.
YOU...
SON OF THE BLUE STAR...
I... UNDERSTAND YOU.

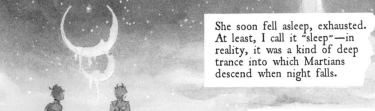

Finally, I was able to make sense of her actions. At great cost to herself, she had spent the first few days of our trek probing my mind in an effort to understand human language.

She soon fell asleep, exhausted. At least, I call it "sleep"—in reality, it was a kind of deep trance into which Martians descend when night falls.

It was the next day that I would discover the princess and her world.

Although the term "princess" may be misleading, it's not entirely inaccurate. She was the youngest of her people and, as such, she was their ruler. At twenty-two Martian years, the princess was the last to emerge from the sacred source from which they were born...

Taking care not to overwhelm my mind, she described her people with images far richer than words. She also transformed water and vapor into a type of fluid puppet theater... I had no doubt that beings capable of such prodigious feats had built a marvelous civilization.

The next morning, she raised her arms in a prayerlike gesture. I was mistaken, though, for the Martians have no gods. Like a flower, she was simply welcoming the sunlight.

The closest things to gods they knew are the canal builders—a people who had disappeared from Mars innumerable generations ago.

I learned that they had launched themselves skyward, leaving strange ruins in the heart of the forbidden deserts. After centuries spent awaiting their return, the Martian civilization was in decline. Their planet was dying, and most of its people had long ago resigned themselves to their fate. But not the princess!

And so, when we arrived, she had been observing the sky.

She came closer cautiously, not daring to probe the minds of these strange beings from space. But, as I found out, her very presence played tricks on human minds...

Until...

Each of us experienced an echo of our desires and our fears...

What happened next, and why they had left without me, she had no way of knowing...

It was in the middle of the night, while she was deep within her strange trance, that we finally reached the entrance to her domain...

OH.

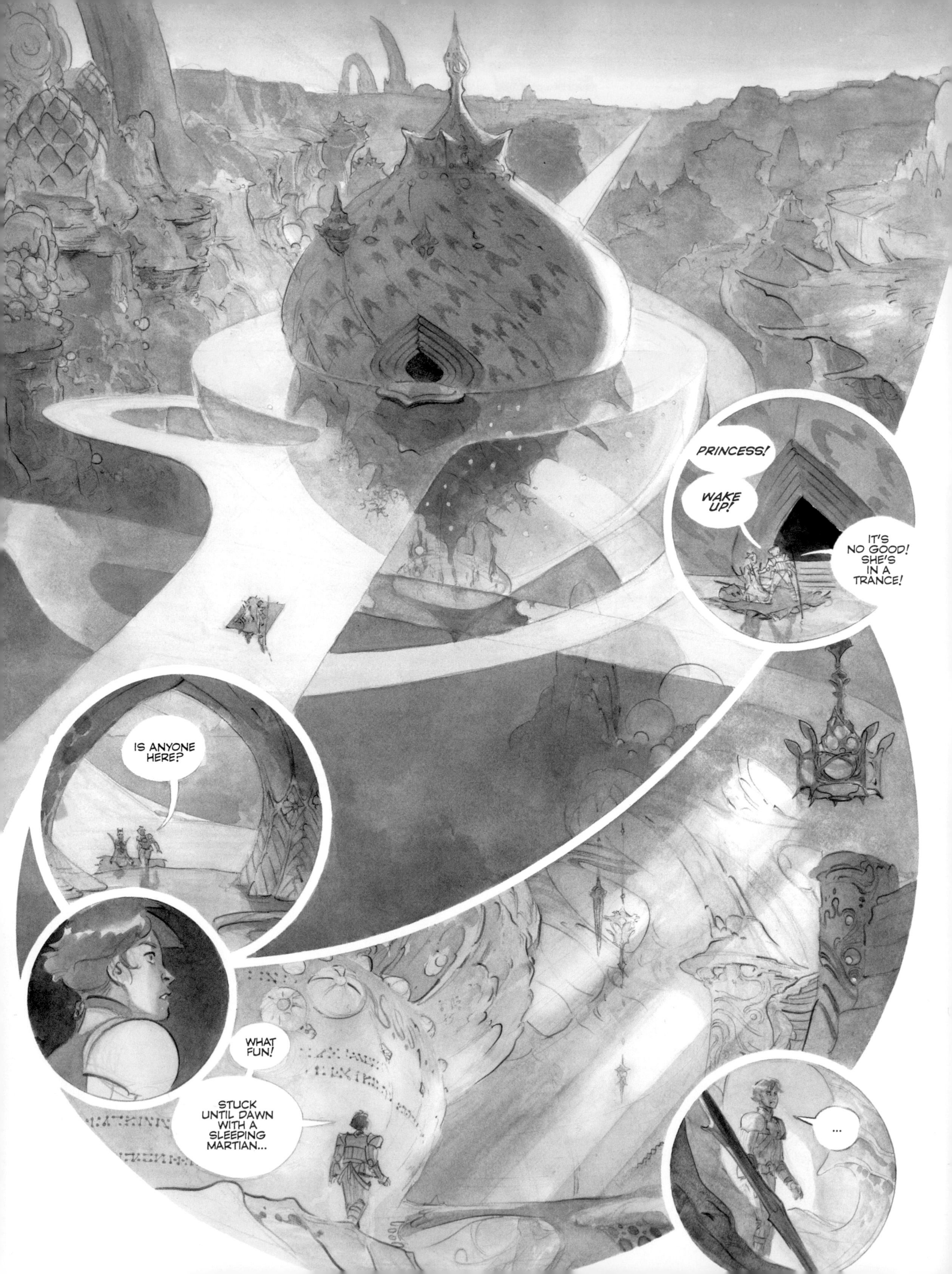
PRINCESS!
WAKE UP!
IT'S NO GOOD! SHE'S IN A TRANCE!
IS ANYONE HERE?
WHAT FUN!
STUCK UNTIL DAWN WITH A SLEEPING MARTIAN...
...

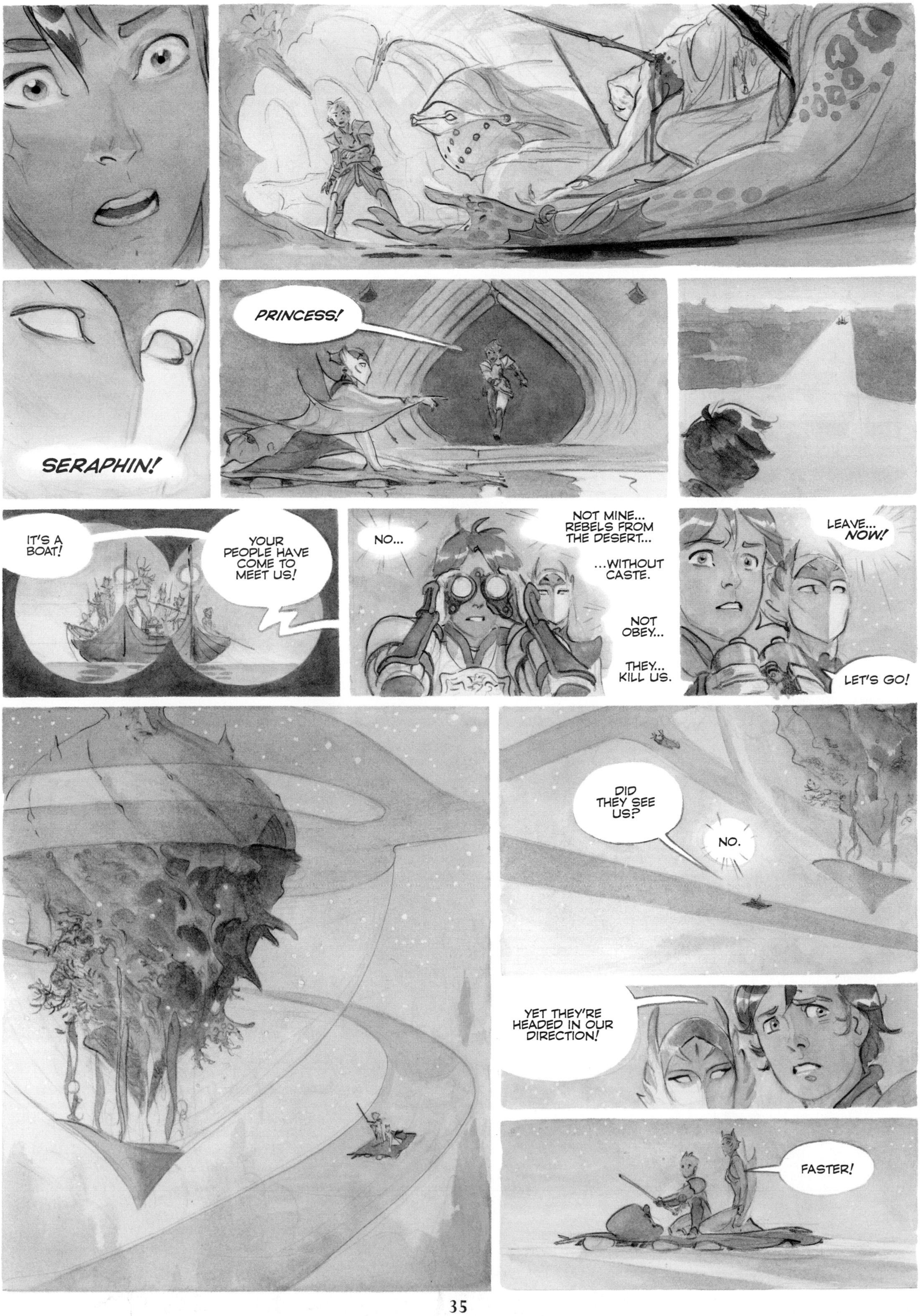
SERAPHIN!
PRINCESS!
IT'S A BOAT!
YOUR PEOPLE HAVE COME TO MEET US!
NO...
NOT MINE... REBELS FROM THE DESERT...
...WITHOUT CASTE.
NOT OBEY...
THEY... KILL US.
LEAVE... NOW!
LET'S GO!
DID THEY SEE US?
NO.
YET THEY'RE HEADED IN OUR DIRECTION!
FASTER!

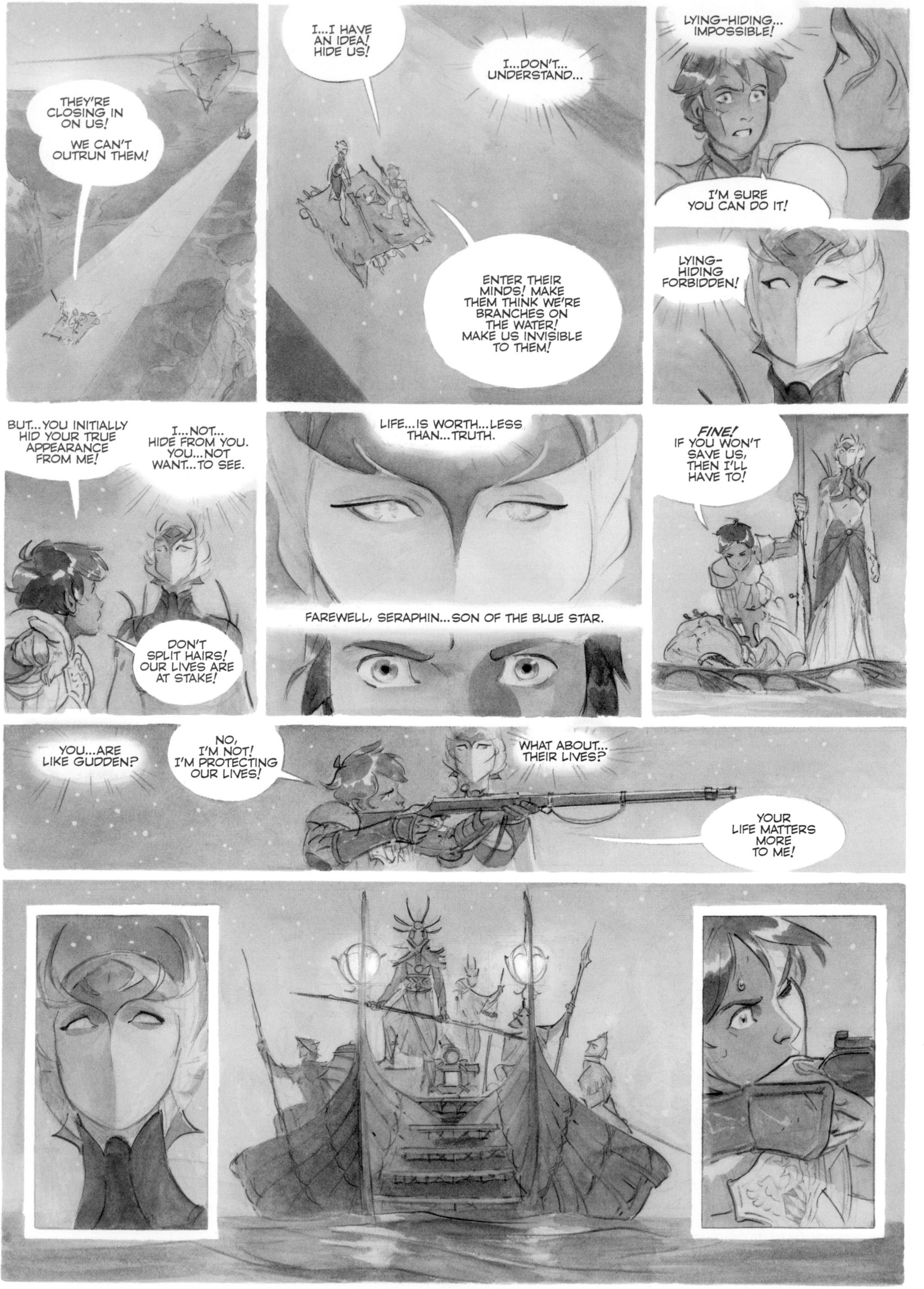
THEY'RE CLOSING IN ON US!
WE CAN'T OUTRUN THEM!
I...I HAVE AN IDEA! HIDE US!
I...DON'T... UNDERSTAND...
ENTER THEIR MINDS! MAKE THEM THINK WE'RE BRANCHES ON THE WATER! MAKE US INVISIBLE TO THEM!
LYING-HIDING... IMPOSSIBLE!
I'M SURE YOU CAN DO IT!
LYING-HIDING FORBIDDEN!
BUT...YOU INITIALLY HID YOUR TRUE APPEARANCE FROM ME!
I...NOT... HIDE FROM YOU. YOU...NOT WANT...TO SEE.
DON'T SPLIT HAIRS! OUR LIVES ARE AT STAKE!
LIFE...IS WORTH...LESS THAN...TRUTH.
FAREWELL, SERAPHIN...SON OF THE BLUE STAR.
FINE! IF YOU WON'T SAVE US, THEN I'LL HAVE TO!
YOU...ARE LIKE GUDDEN?
NO, I'M NOT! I'M PROTECTING OUR LIVES!
WHAT ABOUT... THEIR LIVES?
YOUR LIFE MATTERS MORE TO ME!

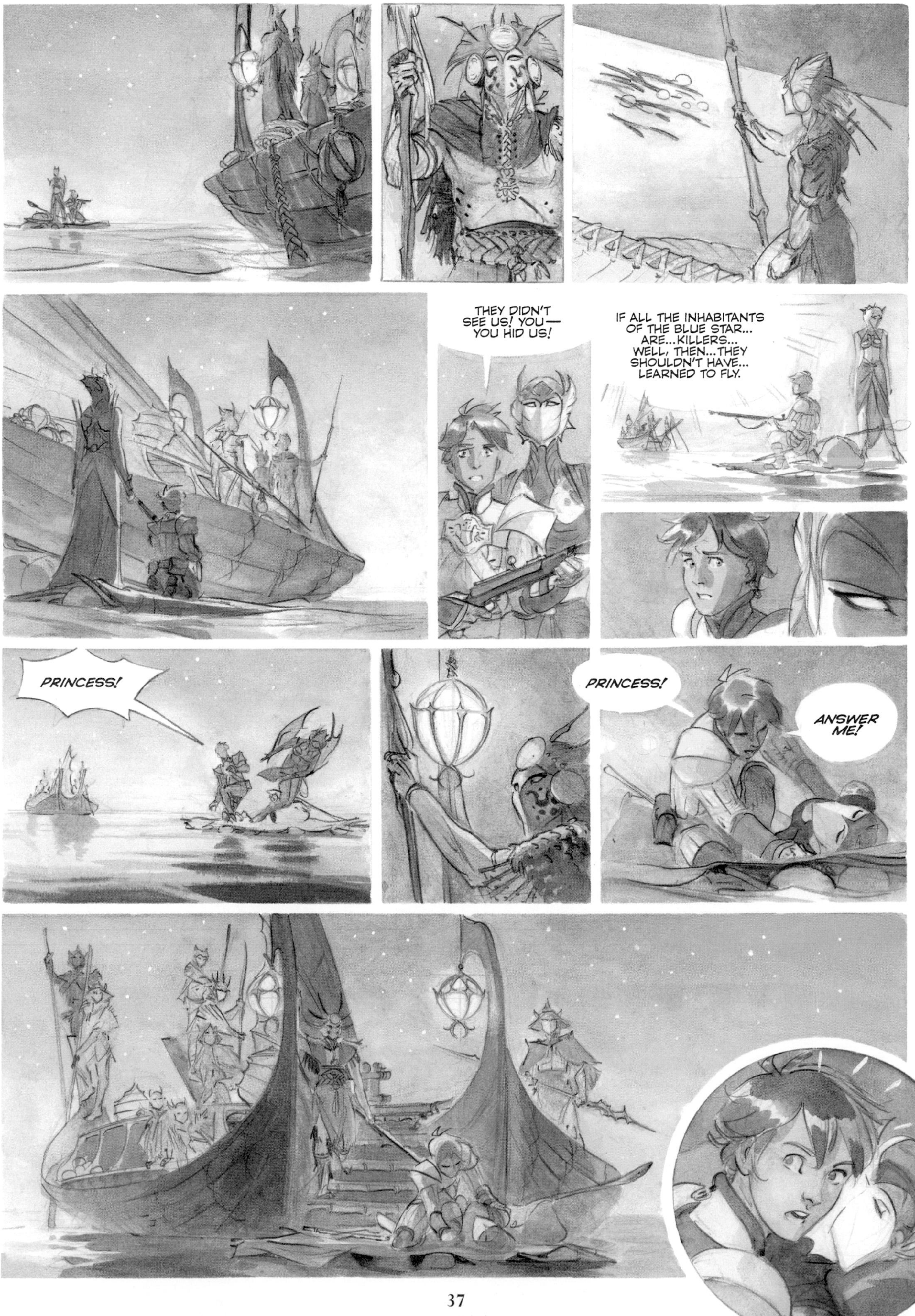
THEY DIDN'T SEE US! YOU— YOU HID US!
IF ALL THE INHABITANTS OF THE BLUE STAR... ARE...KILLERS... WELL, THEN...THEY SHOULDN'T HAVE... LEARNED TO FLY.
PRINCESS!
PRINCESS!
ANSWER ME!

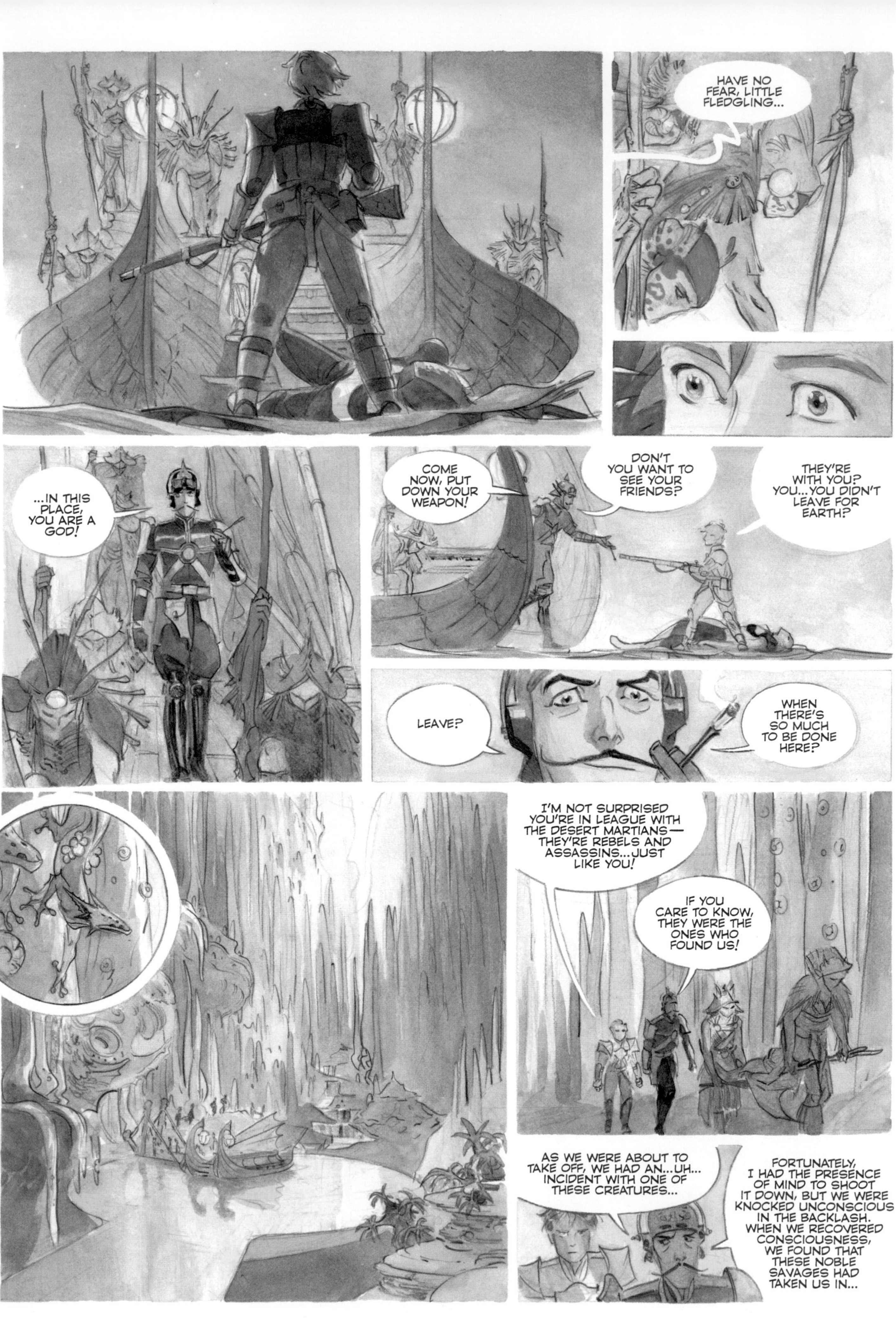
HAVE NO FEAR, LITTLE FLEDGLING...
...IN THIS PLACE, YOU ARE A GOD!
COME NOW, PUT DOWN YOUR WEAPON!
DON'T YOU WANT TO SEE YOUR FRIENDS?
THEY'RE WITH YOU? YOU...YOU DIDN'T LEAVE FOR EARTH?
LEAVE?
WHEN THERE'S SO MUCH TO BE DONE HERE?
I'M NOT SURPRISED YOU'RE IN LEAGUE WITH THE DESERT MARTIANS—THEY'RE REBELS AND ASSASSINS...JUST LIKE YOU!
IF YOU CARE TO KNOW, THEY WERE THE ONES WHO FOUND US!
AS WE WERE ABOUT TO TAKE OFF, WE HAD AN...UH... INCIDENT WITH ONE OF THESE CREATURES...
FORTUNATELY, I HAD THE PRESENCE OF MIND TO SHOOT IT DOWN, BUT WE WERE KNOCKED UNCONSCIOUS IN THE BACKLASH. WHEN WE RECOVERED CONSCIOUSNESS, WE FOUND THAT THESE NOBLE SAVAGES HAD TAKEN US IN...

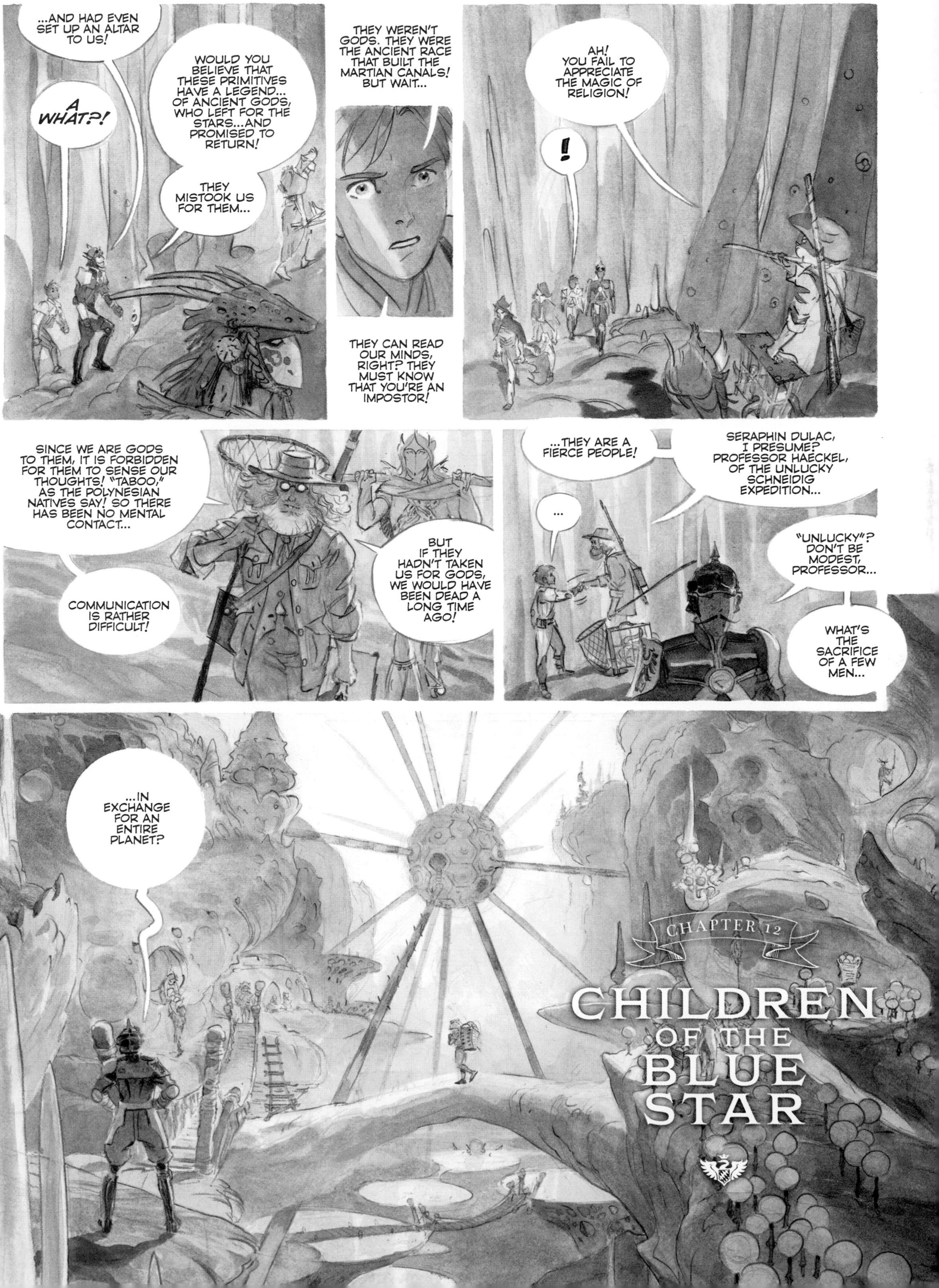
...AND HAD EVEN SET UP AN ALTAR TO US!
A WHAT?!
WOULD YOU BELIEVE THAT THESE PRIMITIVES HAVE A LEGEND... OF ANCIENT GODS, WHO LEFT FOR THE STARS...AND PROMISED TO RETURN!
THEY MISTOOK US FOR THEM...
THEY WEREN'T GODS. THEY WERE THE ANCIENT RACE THAT BUILT THE MARTIAN CANALS! BUT WAIT...
THEY CAN READ OUR MINDS, RIGHT? THEY MUST KNOW THAT YOU'RE AN IMPOSTOR!
AH! YOU FAIL TO APPRECIATE THE MAGIC OF RELIGION!
!
SINCE WE ARE GODS TO THEM, IT IS FORBIDDEN FOR THEM TO SENSE OUR THOUGHTS! "TABOO," AS THE POLYNESIAN NATIVES SAY! SO THERE HAS BEEN NO MENTAL CONTACT...
COMMUNICATION IS RATHER DIFFICULT!
BUT IF THEY HADN'T TAKEN US FOR GODS, WE WOULD HAVE BEEN DEAD A LONG TIME AGO!
...THEY ARE A FIERCE PEOPLE!
...
SERAPHIN DULAC, I PRESUME? PROFESSOR HAECKEL, OF THE UNLUCKY SCHNEIDIG EXPEDITION...
"UNLUCKY"? DON'T BE MODEST, PROFESSOR...
WHAT'S THE SACRIFICE OF A FEW MEN...
...IN EXCHANGE FOR AN ENTIRE PLANET?
CHAPTER 12
CHILDREN OF THE BLUE STAR

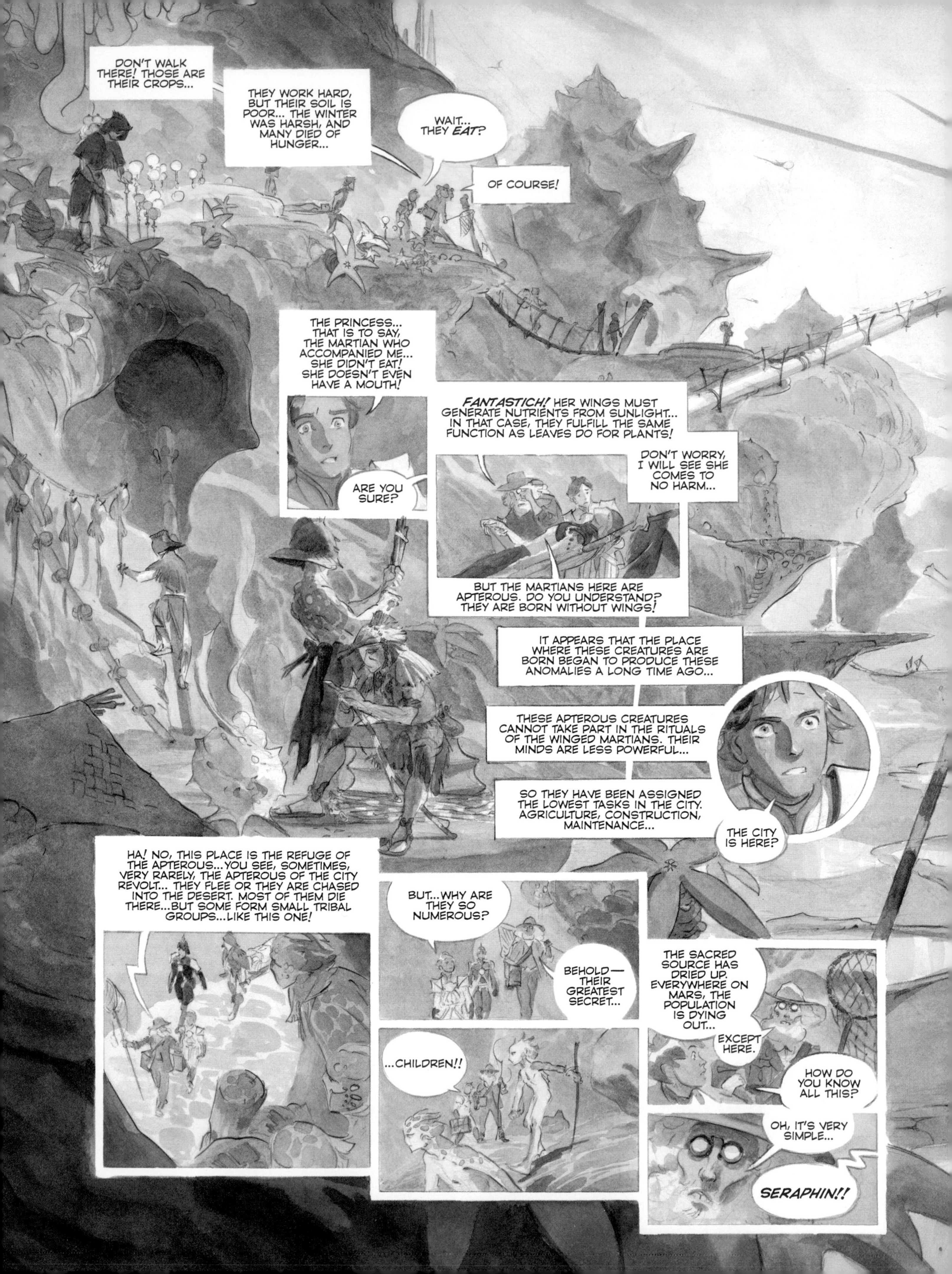
DON'T WALK THERE! THOSE ARE THEIR CROPS...
THEY WORK HARD, BUT THEIR SOIL IS POOR... THE WINTER WAS HARSH, AND MANY DIED OF HUNGER...
WAIT... THEY EAT?
OF COURSE!
THE PRINCESS... THAT IS TO SAY, THE MARTIAN WHO ACCOMPANIED ME... SHE DIDN'T EAT! SHE DOESN'T EVEN HAVE A MOUTH!
ARE YOU SURE?
FANTASTICH! HER WINGS MUST GENERATE NUTRIENTS FROM SUNLIGHT... IN THAT CASE, THEY FULFILL THE SAME FUNCTION AS LEAVES DO FOR PLANTS!
DON'T WORRY, I WILL SEE SHE COMES TO NO HARM...
BUT THE MARTIANS HERE ARE APTEROUS. DO YOU UNDERSTAND? THEY ARE BORN WITHOUT WINGS!
IT APPEARS THAT THE PLACE WHERE THESE CREATURES ARE BORN BEGAN TO PRODUCE THESE ANOMALIES A LONG TIME AGO...
THESE APTEROUS CREATURES CANNOT TAKE PART IN THE RITUALS OF THE WINGED MARTIANS. THEIR MINDS ARE LESS POWERFUL...
SO THEY HAVE BEEN ASSIGNED THE LOWEST TASKS IN THE CITY. AGRICULTURE, CONSTRUCTION, MAINTENANCE...
THE CITY IS HERE?
HA! NO, THIS PLACE IS THE REFUGE OF THE APTEROUS...YOU SEE, SOMETIMES, VERY RARELY, THE APTEROUS OF THE CITY REVOLT... THEY FLEE OR THEY ARE CHASED INTO THE DESERT. MOST OF THEM DIE THERE...BUT SOME FORM SMALL TRIBAL GROUPS...LIKE THIS ONE!
BUT...WHY ARE THEY SO NUMEROUS?
BEHOLD— THEIR GREATEST SECRET...
...CHILDREN!!
THE SACRED SOURCE HAS DRIED UP. EVERYWHERE ON MARS, THE POPULATION IS DYING OUT...
EXCEPT HERE.
HOW DO YOU KNOW ALL THIS?
OH, IT'S VERY SIMPLE...
SERAPHIN!!

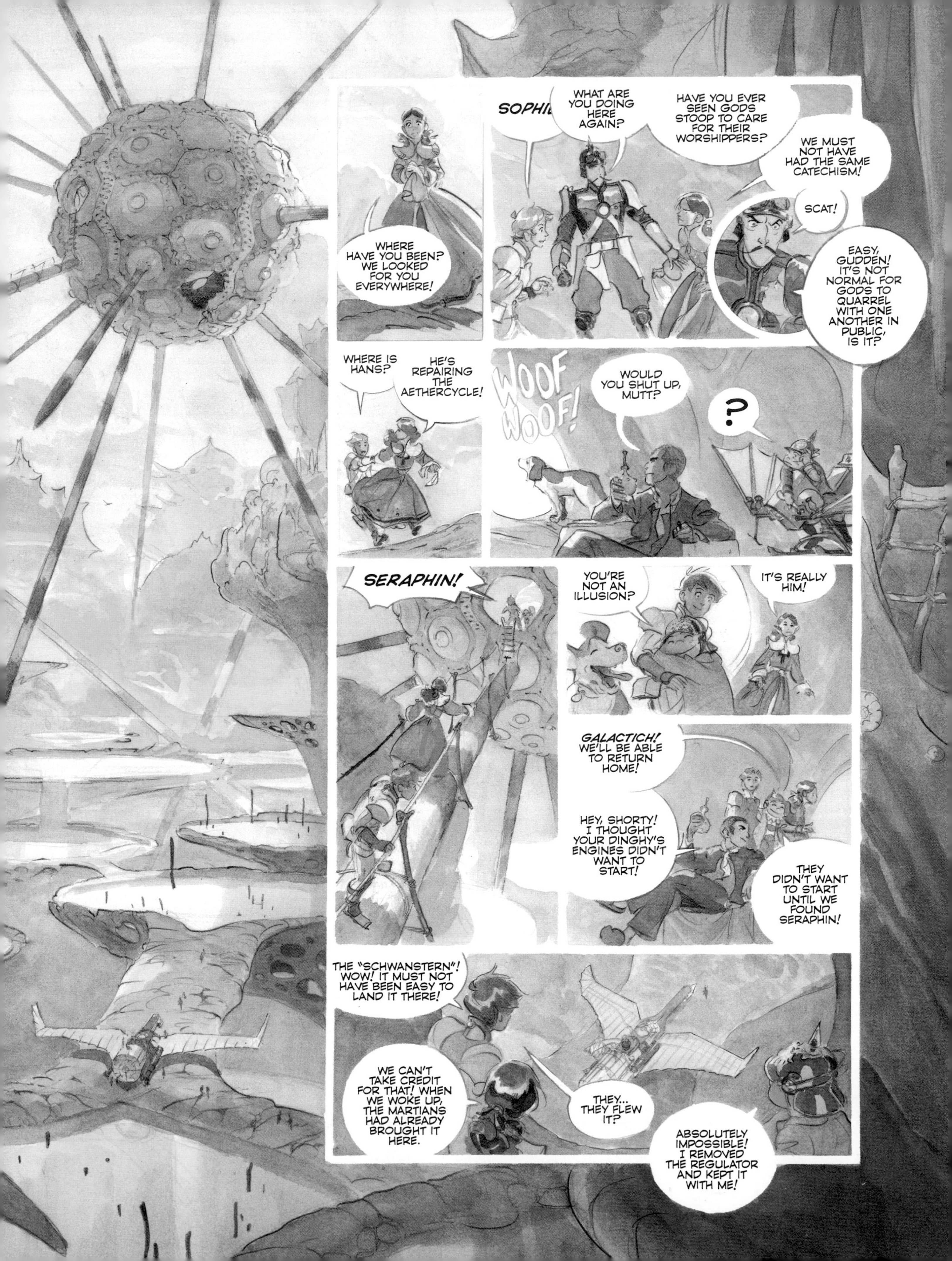
WHERE HAVE YOU BEEN? WE LOOKED FOR YOU EVERYWHERE!
SOPHIE
WHAT ARE YOU DOING HERE AGAIN?
HAVE YOU EVER SEEN GODS STOOP TO CARE FOR THEIR WORSHIPPERS?
WE MUST NOT HAVE HAD THE SAME CATECHISM!
SCAT!
EASY, GUDDEN! IT'S NOT NORMAL FOR GODS TO QUARREL WITH ONE ANOTHER IN PUBLIC, IS IT?
WHERE IS HANS?
HE'S REPAIRING THE AETHERCYCLE!
WOOF WOOF!
WOULD YOU SHUT UP, MUTT?
?
SERAPHIN!
YOU'RE NOT AN ILLUSION?
IT'S REALLY HIM!
GALACTICH! WE'LL BE ABLE TO RETURN HOME!
HEY, SHORTY! I THOUGHT YOUR DINGHY'S ENGINES DIDN'T WANT TO START!
THEY DIDN'T WANT TO START UNTIL WE FOUND SERAPHIN!
THE "SCHWANSTERN"! WOW! IT MUST NOT HAVE BEEN EASY TO LAND IT THERE!
WE CAN'T TAKE CREDIT FOR THAT! WHEN WE WOKE UP, THE MARTIANS HAD ALREADY BROUGHT IT HERE.
THEY... THEY FLEW IT?
ABSOLUTELY IMPOSSIBLE! I REMOVED THE REGULATOR AND KEPT IT WITH ME!

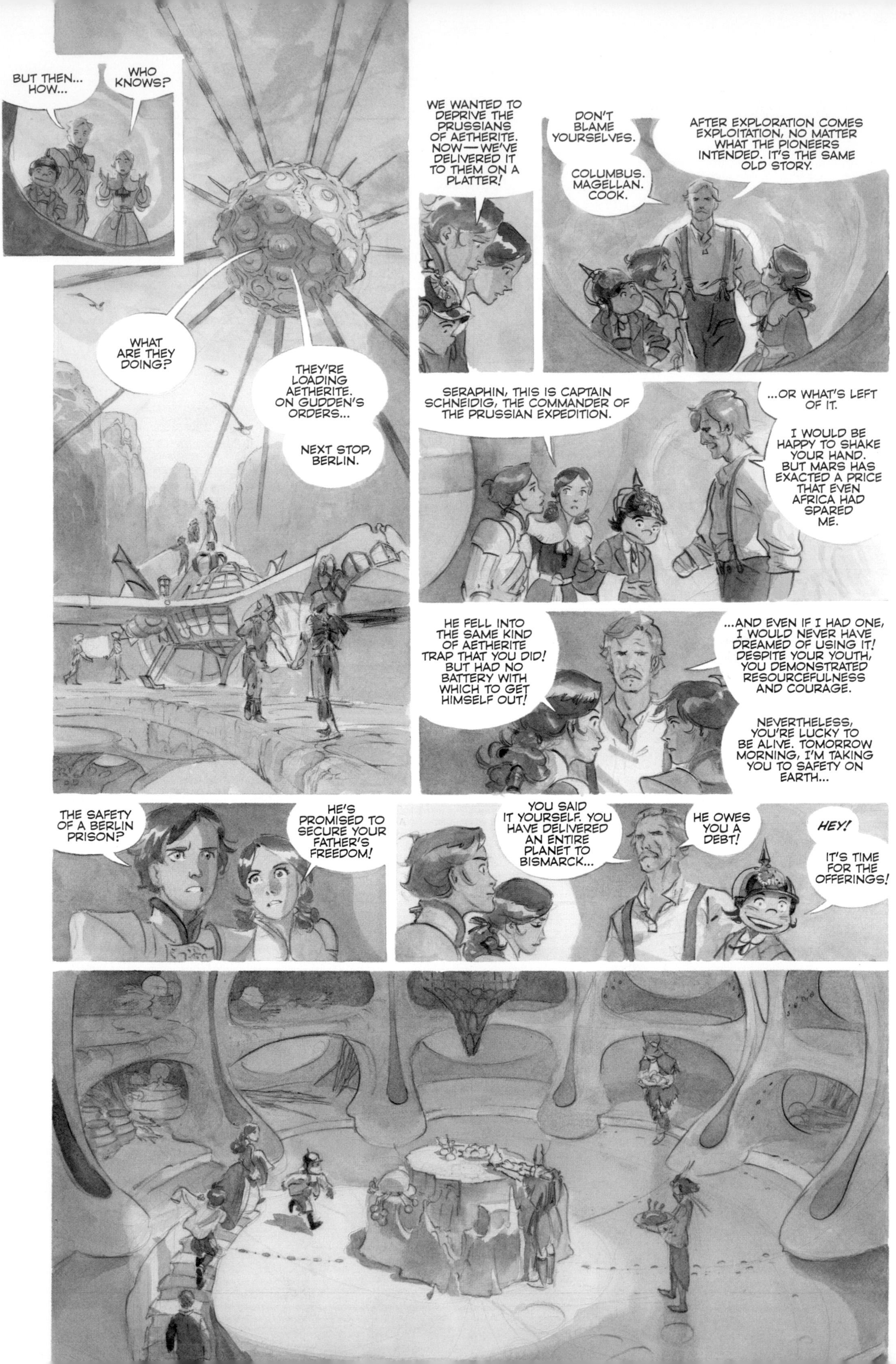
BUT THEN... HOW...
WHO KNOWS?
WHAT ARE THEY DOING?
THEY'RE LOADING AETHERITE. ON GUDDEN'S ORDERS...
NEXT STOP, BERLIN.
WE WANTED TO DEPRIVE THE PRUSSIANS OF AETHERITE. NOW—WE'VE DELIVERED IT TO THEM ON A PLATTER!
DON'T BLAME YOURSELVES.
COLUMBUS. MAGELLAN. COOK.
AFTER EXPLORATION COMES EXPLOITATION, NO MATTER WHAT THE PIONEERS INTENDED. IT'S THE SAME OLD STORY.
SERAPHIN, THIS IS CAPTAIN SCHNEIDIG, THE COMMANDER OF THE PRUSSIAN EXPEDITION.
...OR WHAT'S LEFT OF IT.
I WOULD BE HAPPY TO SHAKE YOUR HAND. BUT MARS HAS EXACTED A PRICE THAT EVEN AFRICA HAD SPARED ME.
HE FELL INTO THE SAME KIND OF AETHERITE TRAP THAT YOU DID! BUT HAD NO BATTERY WITH WHICH TO GET HIMSELF OUT!
...AND EVEN IF I HAD ONE, I WOULD NEVER HAVE DREAMED OF USING IT! DESPITE YOUR YOUTH, YOU DEMONSTRATED RESOURCEFULNESS AND COURAGE.
NEVERTHELESS, YOU'RE LUCKY TO BE ALIVE. TOMORROW MORNING, I'M TAKING YOU TO SAFETY ON EARTH...
THE SAFETY OF A BERLIN PRISON?
HE'S PROMISED TO SECURE YOUR FATHER'S FREEDOM!
YOU SAID IT YOURSELF. YOU HAVE DELIVERED AN ENTIRE PLANET TO BISMARCK...
HE OWES YOU A DEBT!
HEY!
IT'S TIME FOR THE OFFERINGS!

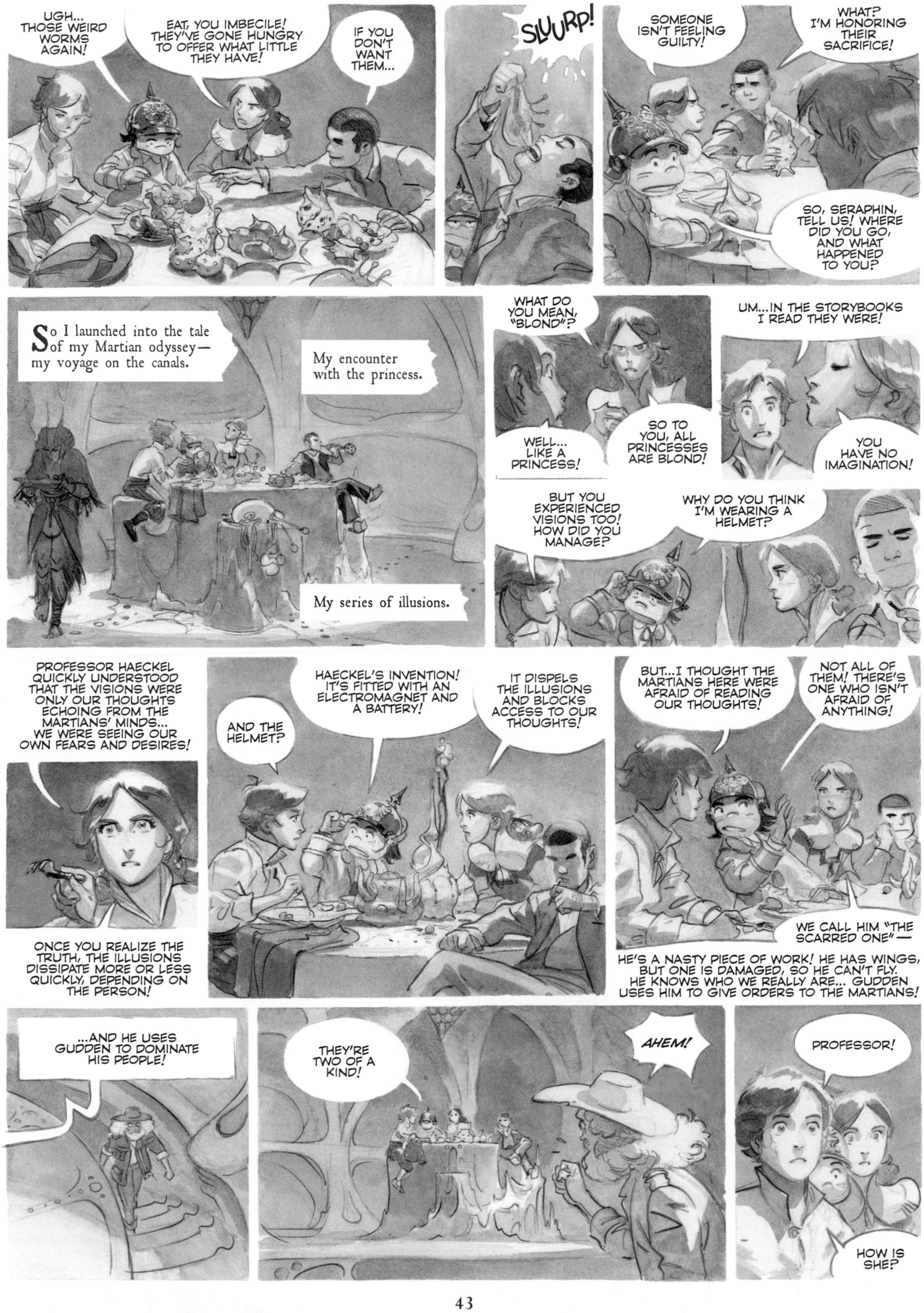
UGH... THOSE WEIRD WORMS AGAIN!
EAT, YOU IMBECILE! THEY'VE GONE HUNGRY TO OFFER WHAT LITTLE THEY HAVE!
IF YOU DON'T WANT THEM...
SLUURP!
SOMEONE ISN'T FEELING GUILTY!
WHAT? I'M HONORING THEIR SACRIFICE!
SO, SERAPHIN, TELL US! WHERE DID YOU GO, AND WHAT HAPPENED TO YOU?
So I launched into the tale of my Martian odyssey—my voyage on the canals.
My encounter with the princess.
My series of illusions.
WHAT DO YOU MEAN, "BLOND"?
WELL... LIKE A PRINCESS!
SO TO YOU, ALL PRINCESSES ARE BLOND!
UM...IN THE STORYBOOKS I READ THEY WERE!
YOU HAVE NO IMAGINATION!
BUT YOU EXPERIENCED VISIONS TOO! HOW DID YOU MANAGE?
WHY DO YOU THINK I'M WEARING A HELMET?
PROFESSOR HAECKEL QUICKLY UNDERSTOOD THAT THE VISIONS WERE ONLY OUR THOUGHTS ECHOING FROM THE MARTIANS' MINDS... WE WERE SEEING OUR OWN FEARS AND DESIRES!
ONCE YOU REALIZE THE TRUTH, THE ILLUSIONS DISSIPATE MORE OR LESS QUICKLY, DEPENDING ON THE PERSON!
AND THE HELMET?
HAECKEL'S INVENTION! IT'S FITTED WITH AN ELECTROMAGNET AND A BATTERY!
IT DISPELS THE ILLUSIONS AND BLOCKS ACCESS TO OUR THOUGHTS!
BUT...I THOUGHT THE MARTIANS HERE WERE AFRAID OF READING OUR THOUGHTS!
NOT ALL OF THEM! THERE'S ONE WHO ISN'T AFRAID OF ANYTHING!
WE CALL HIM "THE SCARRED ONE"—
HE'S A NASTY PIECE OF WORK! HE HAS WINGS, BUT ONE IS DAMAGED, SO HE CAN'T FLY. HE KNOWS WHO WE REALLY ARE... GUDDEN USES HIM TO GIVE ORDERS TO THE MARTIANS!
...AND HE USES GUDDEN TO DOMINATE HIS PEOPLE!
THEY'RE TWO OF A KIND!
AHEM!
PROFESSOR!
HOW IS SHE?

I'M AFRAID HER VITAL SIGNS ARE SLOWLY FADING...

IT MIGHT BE THE WOUND, BUT I DON'T THINK SO. ANYWAY, WE'LL FIND OUT AT THE AUTOPSY.

?!

THE AUTOPSY?!

YES. I DON'T THINK SHE'LL SURVIVE THE NIGHT.

A SHAME...

ALIVE, SHE WOULD HAVE MADE A VALUABLE PRISONER.

BUT...CAN'T THE MARTIANS CURE HER?

THE ONES HERE? THEY DETEST THE WINGED ONES! IF SHE WEREN'T UNDER OUR PROTECTION, THEY WOULD HAVE ALREADY KILLED HER!

THEN LET ME TAKE HER BACK HOME! HER OWN PEOPLE WILL SAVE HER!

NO.

PROFESSOR... ONCE SHE'S DEAD, PREPARE THE BODY.

!

TOMORROW, WE SHALL RETURN TO EARTH WITH A TROPHY FOR BISMARCK!

YOU'RE MAD! WE MUST SAVE HER!

LIEUTENANT...

I'M ON IT, SIR!

AAAH!

CONFINE THEM UNTIL WE LEAVE. I DON'T WANT ANY UNPLEASANT SURPRISES.

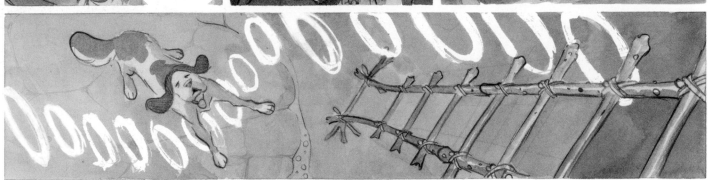

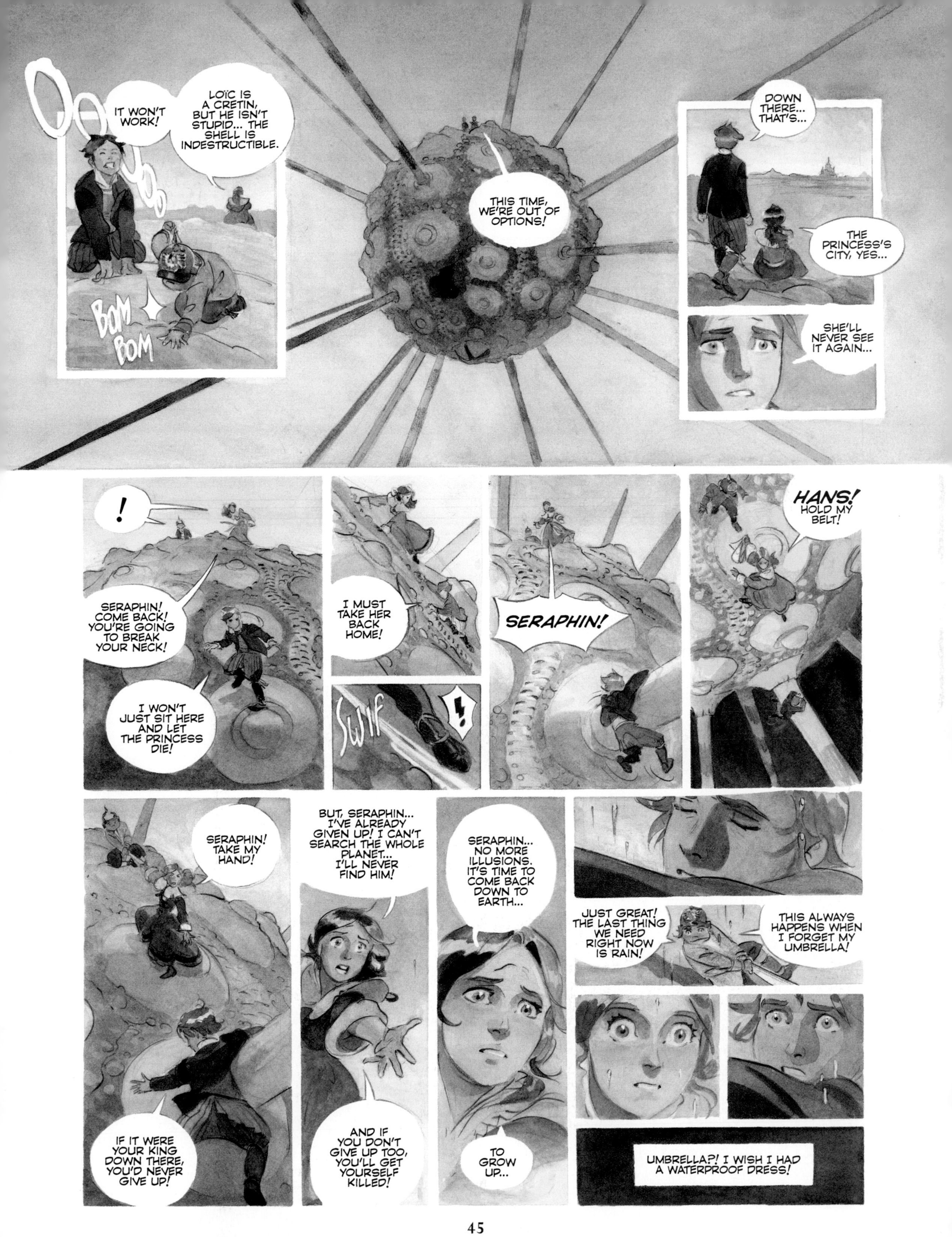
IT WON'T WORK!
LOÏC IS A CRETIN, BUT HE ISN'T STUPID... THE SHELL IS INDESTRUCTIBLE.
BOM BOM
THIS TIME, WE'RE OUT OF OPTIONS!
DOWN THERE... THAT'S...
THE PRINCESS'S CITY, YES...
SHE'LL NEVER SEE IT AGAIN...
!
SERAPHIN! COME BACK! YOU'RE GOING TO BREAK YOUR NECK!
I WON'T JUST SIT HERE AND LET THE PRINCESS DIE!
I MUST TAKE HER BACK HOME!
SWIF
!
SERAPHIN!
HANS! HOLD MY BELT!
SERAPHIN! TAKE MY HAND!
IF IT WERE YOUR KING DOWN THERE, YOU'D NEVER GIVE UP!
BUT, SERAPHIN... I'VE ALREADY GIVEN UP! I CAN'T SEARCH THE WHOLE PLANET... I'LL NEVER FIND HIM!
AND IF YOU DON'T GIVE UP TOO, YOU'LL GET YOURSELF KILLED!
SERAPHIN... NO MORE ILLUSIONS. IT'S TIME TO COME BACK DOWN TO EARTH...
TO GROW UP...
JUST GREAT! THE LAST THING WE NEED RIGHT NOW IS RAIN!
THIS ALWAYS HAPPENS WHEN I FORGET MY UMBRELLA!
UMBRELLA?! I WISH I HAD A WATERPROOF DRESS!

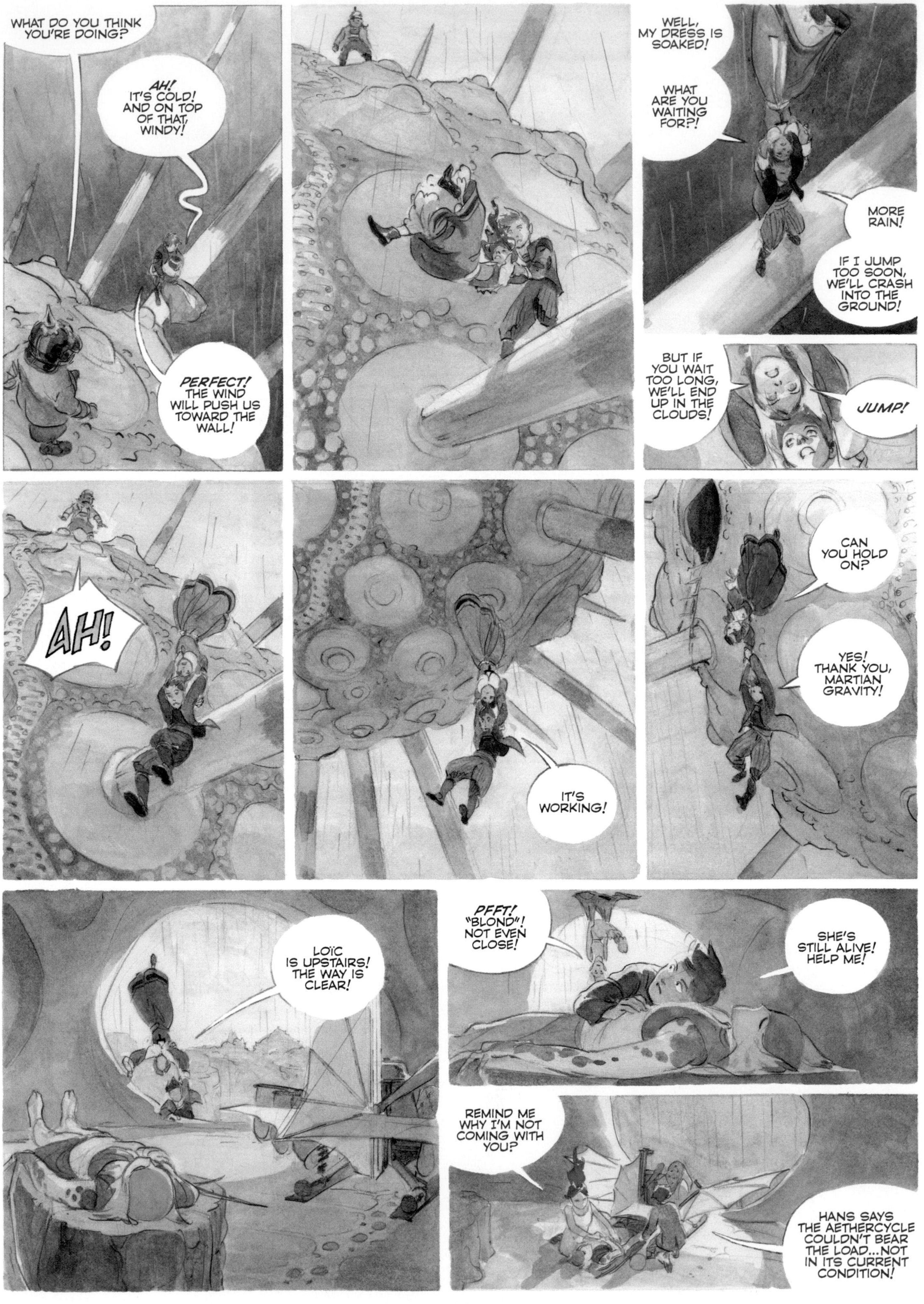
WHAT DO YOU THINK YOU'RE DOING?
AH! IT'S COLD! AND ON TOP OF THAT, WINDY!
PERFECT! THE WIND WILL PUSH US TOWARD THE WALL!
WELL, MY DRESS IS SOAKED!
WHAT ARE YOU WAITING FOR?!
MORE RAIN!
IF I JUMP TOO SOON, WE'LL CRASH INTO THE GROUND!
BUT IF YOU WAIT TOO LONG, WE'LL END UP IN THE CLOUDS!
JUMP!
AH!
IT'S WORKING!
CAN YOU HOLD ON?
YES! THANK YOU, MARTIAN GRAVITY!
LOÏC IS UPSTAIRS! THE WAY IS CLEAR!
PFFT! "BLOND"! NOT EVEN CLOSE!
SHE'S STILL ALIVE! HELP ME!
REMIND ME WHY I'M NOT COMING WITH YOU?
HANS SAYS THE AETHERCYCLE COULDN'T BEAR THE LOAD...NOT IN ITS CURRENT CONDITION!

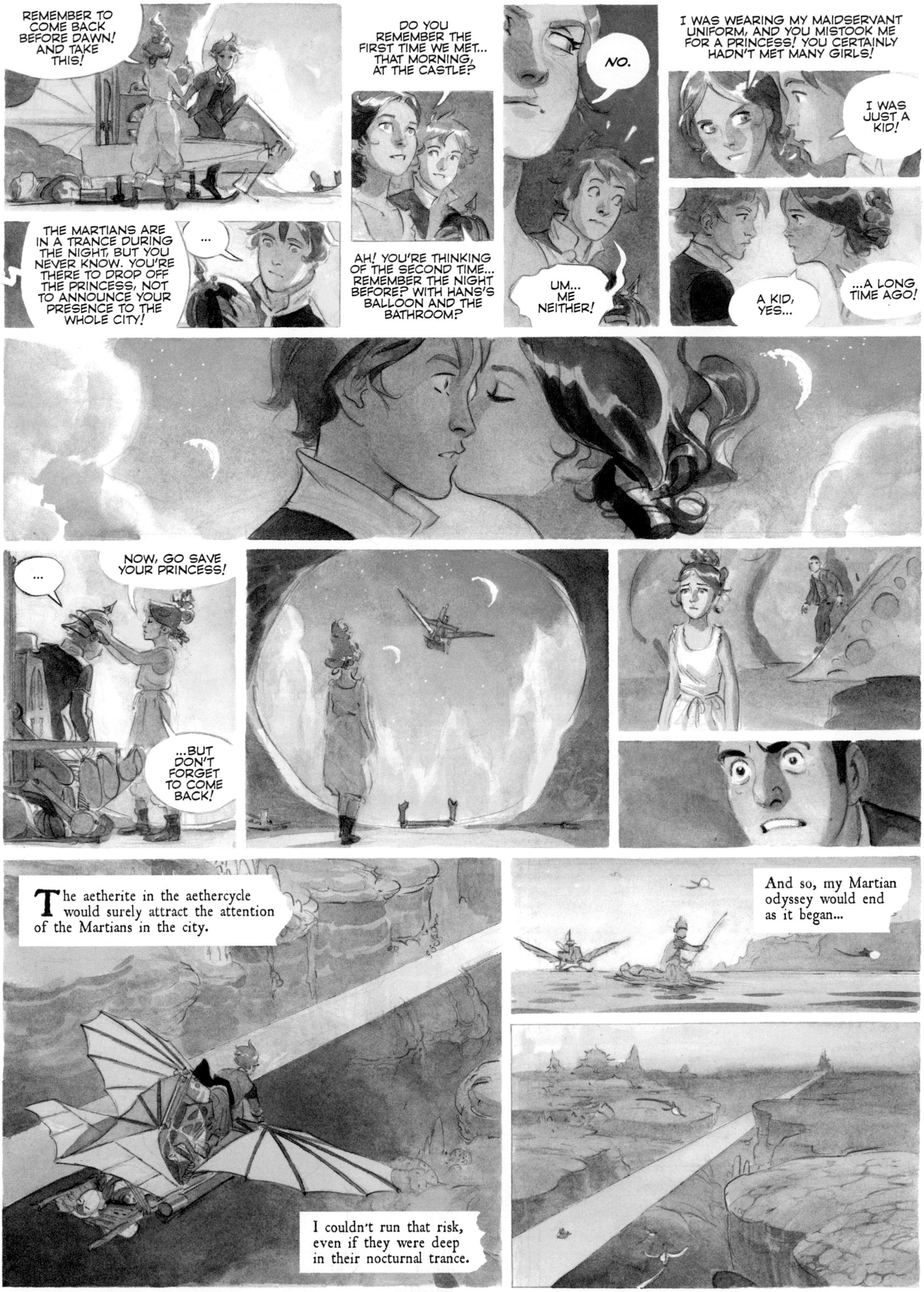
REMEMBER TO COME BACK BEFORE DAWN! AND TAKE THIS!
THE MARTIANS ARE IN A TRANCE DURING THE NIGHT, BUT YOU NEVER KNOW. YOU'RE THERE TO DROP OFF THE PRINCESS, NOT TO ANNOUNCE YOUR PRESENCE TO THE WHOLE CITY!
...
DO YOU REMEMBER THE FIRST TIME WE MET... THAT MORNING, AT THE CASTLE?
AH! YOU'RE THINKING OF THE SECOND TIME... REMEMBER THE NIGHT BEFORE? WITH HANS'S BALLOON AND THE BATHROOM?
NO.
UM... ME NEITHER!
I WAS WEARING MY MAIDSERVANT UNIFORM, AND YOU MISTOOK ME FOR A PRINCESS! YOU CERTAINLY HADN'T MET MANY GIRLS!
I WAS JUST A KID!
A KID, YES...
...A LONG TIME AGO!
...
NOW, GO SAVE YOUR PRINCESS!
...BUT DON'T FORGET TO COME BACK!
The aetherite in the aethercycle would surely attract the attention of the Martians in the city.
I couldn't run that risk, even if they were deep in their nocturnal trance.
And so, my Martian odyssey would end as it began...

CLACK!

HEY!

NOT ONE WORD, IMBECILE! YOU LET THAT KID ESCAPE— NOW HE'LL RUIN EVERYTHING!

PREPARE MY ARMOR— WE ATTACK TONIGHT!

LOÏC!

WHAT DID HE MEAN?

ATTACK WHAT?

USE YOUR HEAD, SILLY GIRL!

DID YOU REALLY THINK THAT GUDDEN AND I WOULD QUIETLY RETURN TO OUR POSITIONS ON EARTH? WE ARE GODS HERE! WITH AN ARMY AT OUR DISPOSAL!

AN ARMY?

THE APTEROUS, YOU IDIOT! THEY'RE READY TO MARCH ON THE PRINCESS'S CITY! FROM THERE, WE CAN CONQUER THE WHOLE PLANET! SCHNEIDIG WAS SUPPOSED TO RETURN TO EARTH TO SEEK REINFORCEMENTS...

GETTING RID OF US IN THE PROCESS!

UNLESS YOU WANT TO STAY! I CAN BE PERSUADED, YOU KNOW!

WHERE IS THAT ARMOR?!

BEST HEED YOUR MASTER'S WHISTLE, GREAT GOD OF MARS!

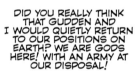

!

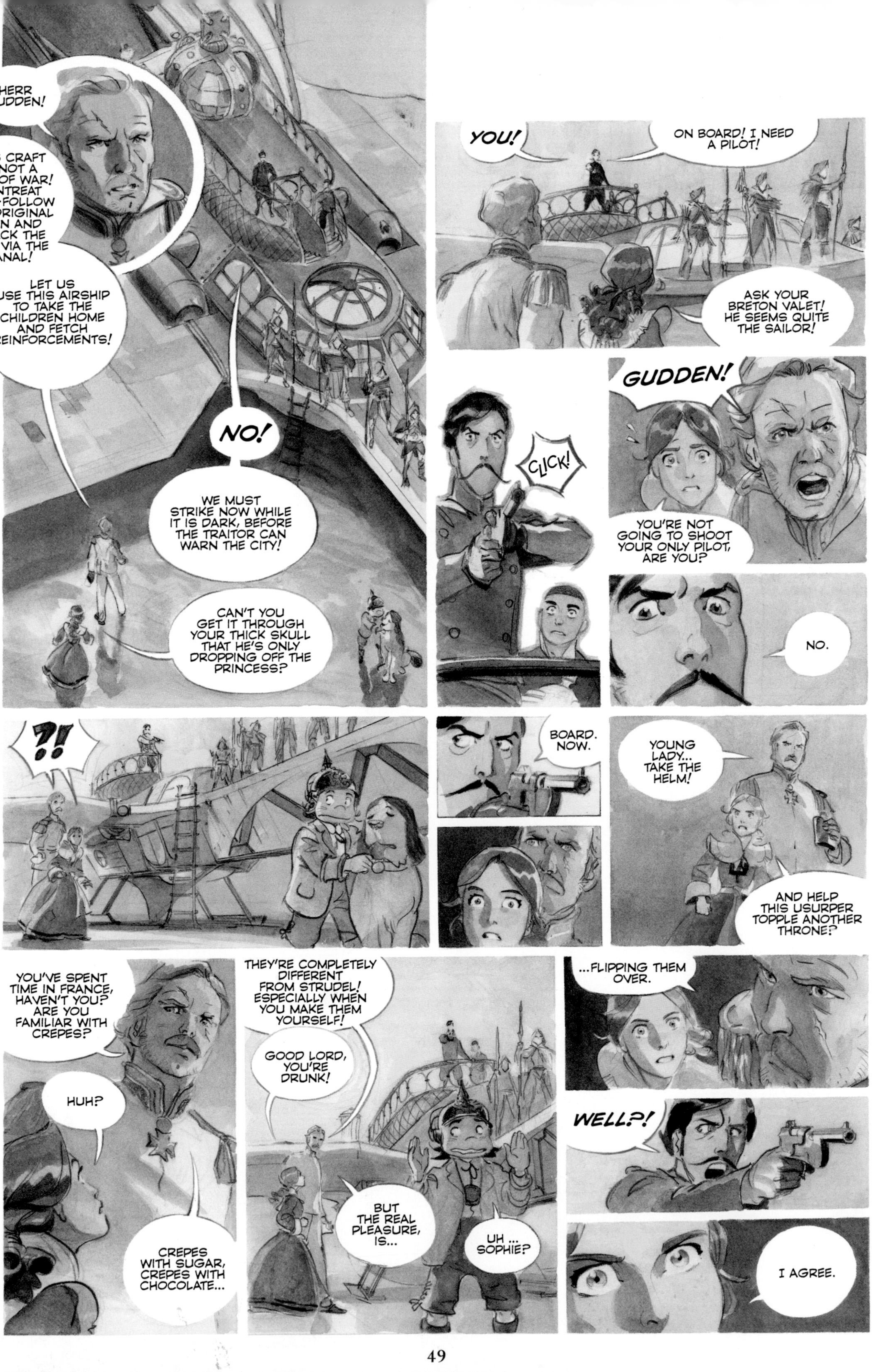
HERR GUDDEN!
THIS CRAFT IS NOT A SHIP OF WAR! I ENTREAT YOU—FOLLOW THE ORIGINAL PLAN AND ATTACK THE CITY VIA THE CANAL!
LET US USE THIS AIRSHIP TO TAKE THE CHILDREN HOME AND FETCH REINFORCEMENTS!
NO!
WE MUST STRIKE NOW WHILE IT IS DARK, BEFORE THE TRAITOR CAN WARN THE CITY!
CAN'T YOU GET IT THROUGH YOUR THICK SKULL THAT HE'S ONLY DROPPING OFF THE PRINCESS?
YOU!
ON BOARD! I NEED A PILOT!
ASK YOUR BRETON VALET! HE SEEMS QUITE THE SAILOR!
CLICK!
GUDDEN!
YOU'RE NOT GOING TO SHOOT YOUR ONLY PILOT, ARE YOU?
NO.
?!
BOARD. NOW.
YOUNG LADY... TAKE THE HELM!
AND HELP THIS USURPER TOPPLE ANOTHER THRONE?
YOU'VE SPENT TIME IN FRANCE, HAVEN'T YOU? ARE YOU FAMILIAR WITH CREPES?
HUH?
CREPES WITH SUGAR, CREPES WITH CHOCOLATE...
THEY'RE COMPLETELY DIFFERENT FROM STRUDEL! ESPECIALLY WHEN YOU MAKE THEM YOURSELF!
GOOD LORD, YOU'RE DRUNK!
BUT THE REAL PLEASURE, IS...
UH ... SOPHIE?
...FLIPPING THEM OVER.
WELL?!
I AGREE.

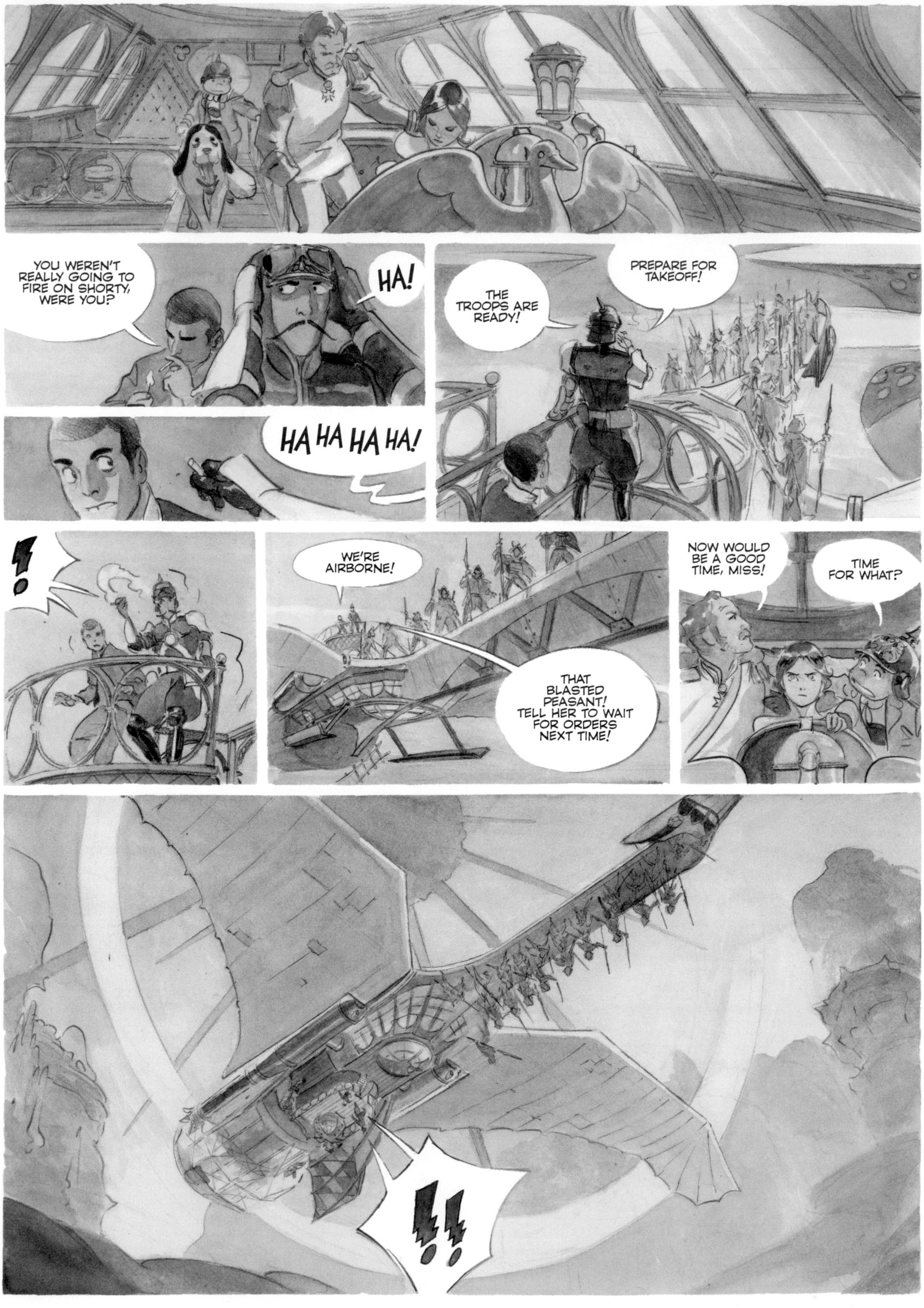
YOU WEREN'T REALLY GOING TO FIRE ON SHORTY, WERE YOU?
HA!
THE TROOPS ARE READY!
PREPARE FOR TAKEOFF!
HA HA HA HA!
!
WE'RE AIRBORNE!
THAT BLASTED PEASANT! TELL HER TO WAIT FOR ORDERS NEXT TIME!
NOW WOULD BE A GOOD TIME, MISS!
TIME FOR WHAT?
!!

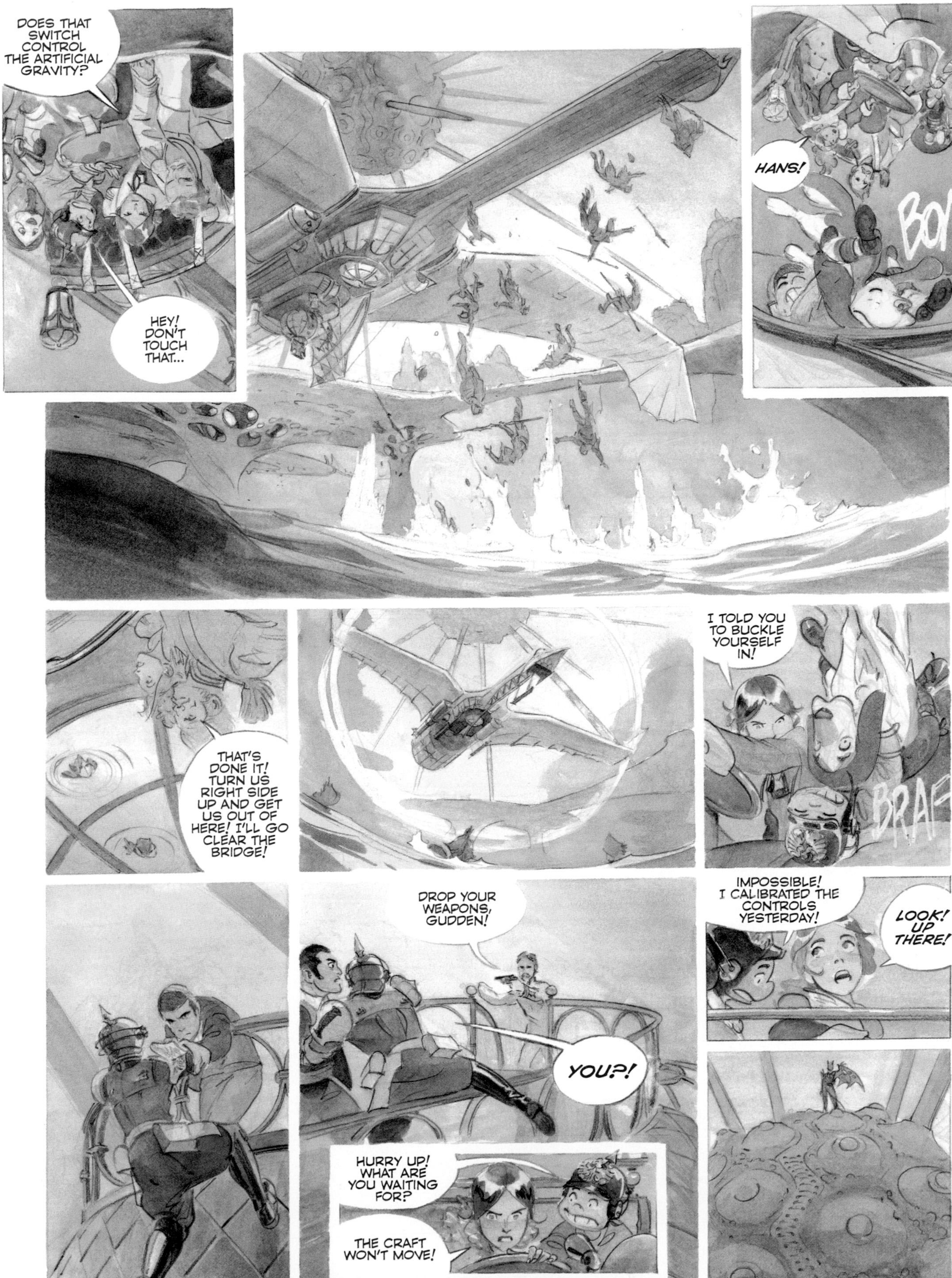
DOES THAT SWITCH CONTROL THE ARTIFICIAL GRAVITY?
HEY! DON'T TOUCH THAT...
HANS!
BONG
THAT'S DONE IT! TURN US RIGHT SIDE UP AND GET US OUT OF HERE! I'LL GO CLEAR THE BRIDGE!
I TOLD YOU TO BUCKLE YOURSELF IN!
BRAF
DROP YOUR WEAPONS, GUDDEN!
YOU?!
HURRY UP! WHAT ARE YOU WAITING FOR?
THE CRAFT WON'T MOVE!
IMPOSSIBLE! I CALIBRATED THE CONTROLS YESTERDAY!
LOOK! UP THERE!

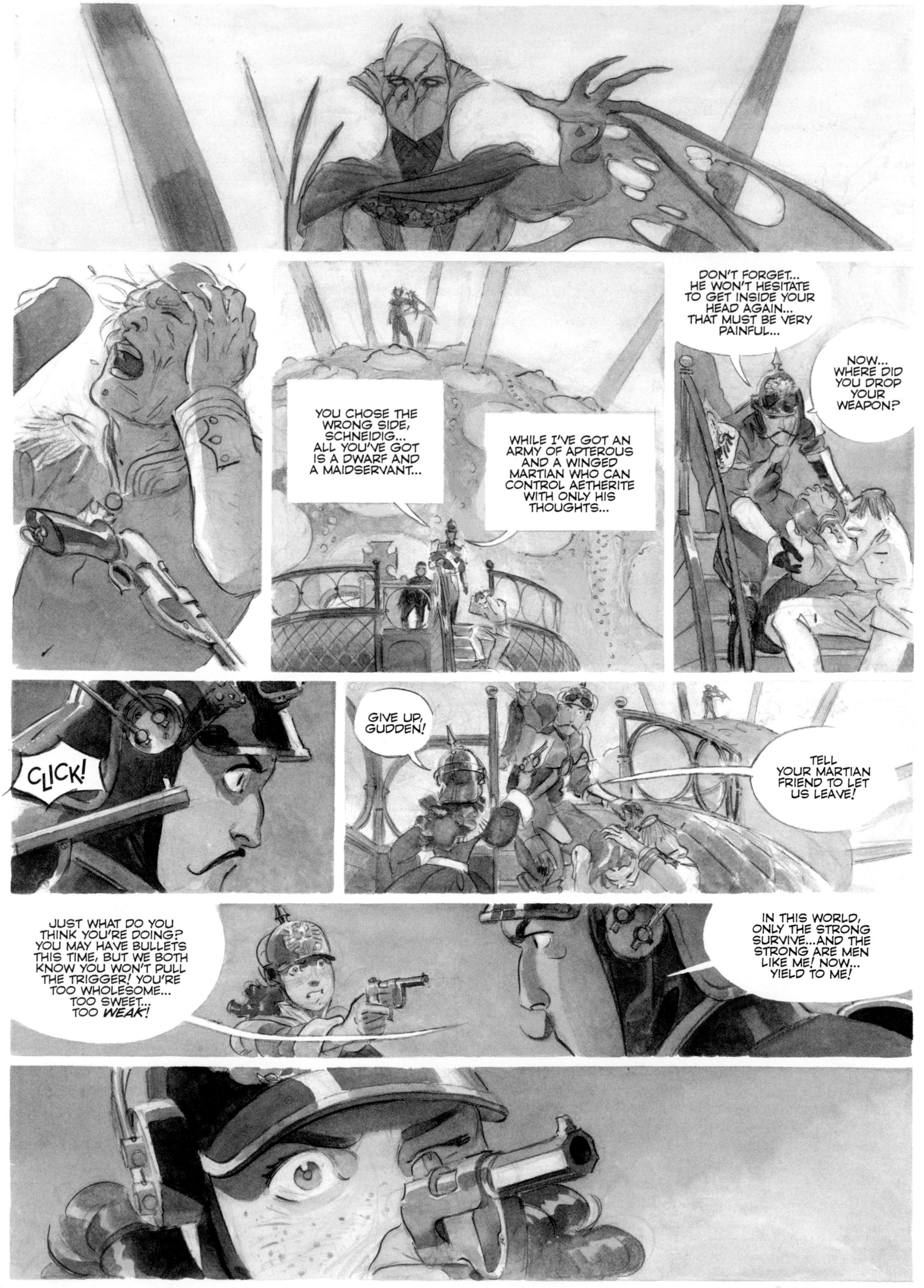
YOU CHOSE THE WRONG SIDE, SCHNEIDIG... ALL YOU'VE GOT IS A DWARF AND A MAIDSERVANT...
WHILE I'VE GOT AN ARMY OF APTEROUS AND A WINGED MARTIAN WHO CAN CONTROL AETHERITE WITH ONLY HIS THOUGHTS...
DON'T FORGET... HE WON'T HESITATE TO GET INSIDE YOUR HEAD AGAIN... THAT MUST BE VERY PAINFUL...
NOW... WHERE DID YOU DROP YOUR WEAPON?
CLICK!
GIVE UP, GUDDEN!
TELL YOUR MARTIAN FRIEND TO LET US LEAVE!
JUST WHAT DO YOU THINK YOU'RE DOING? YOU MAY HAVE BULLETS THIS TIME, BUT WE BOTH KNOW YOU WON'T PULL THE TRIGGER! YOU'RE TOO WHOLESOME... TOO SWEET... TOO WEAK!
IN THIS WORLD, ONLY THE STRONG SURVIVE...AND THE STRONG ARE MEN LIKE ME! NOW... YIELD TO ME!

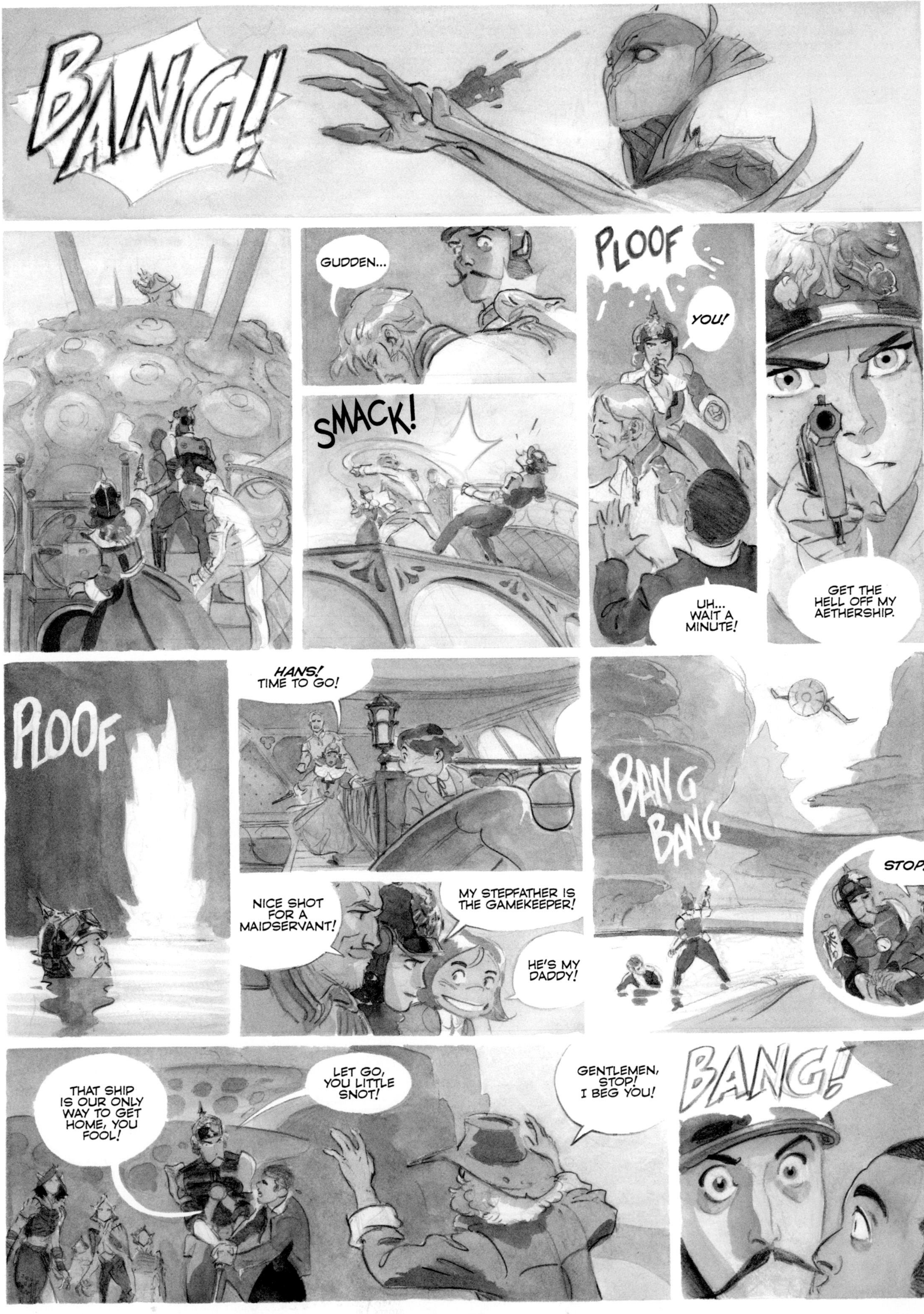
BANG!
GUDDEN...
SMACK!
PLOOF
YOU!
UH... WAIT A MINUTE!
GET THE HELL OFF MY AETHERSHIP.
PLOOF
HANS! TIME TO GO!
NICE SHOT FOR A MAIDSERVANT!
MY STEPFATHER IS THE GAMEKEEPER!
HE'S MY DADDY!
BANG BANG
STOP!
THAT SHIP IS OUR ONLY WAY TO GET HOME, YOU FOOL!
LET GO, YOU LITTLE SNOT!
GENTLEMEN, STOP! I BEG YOU!
BANG!

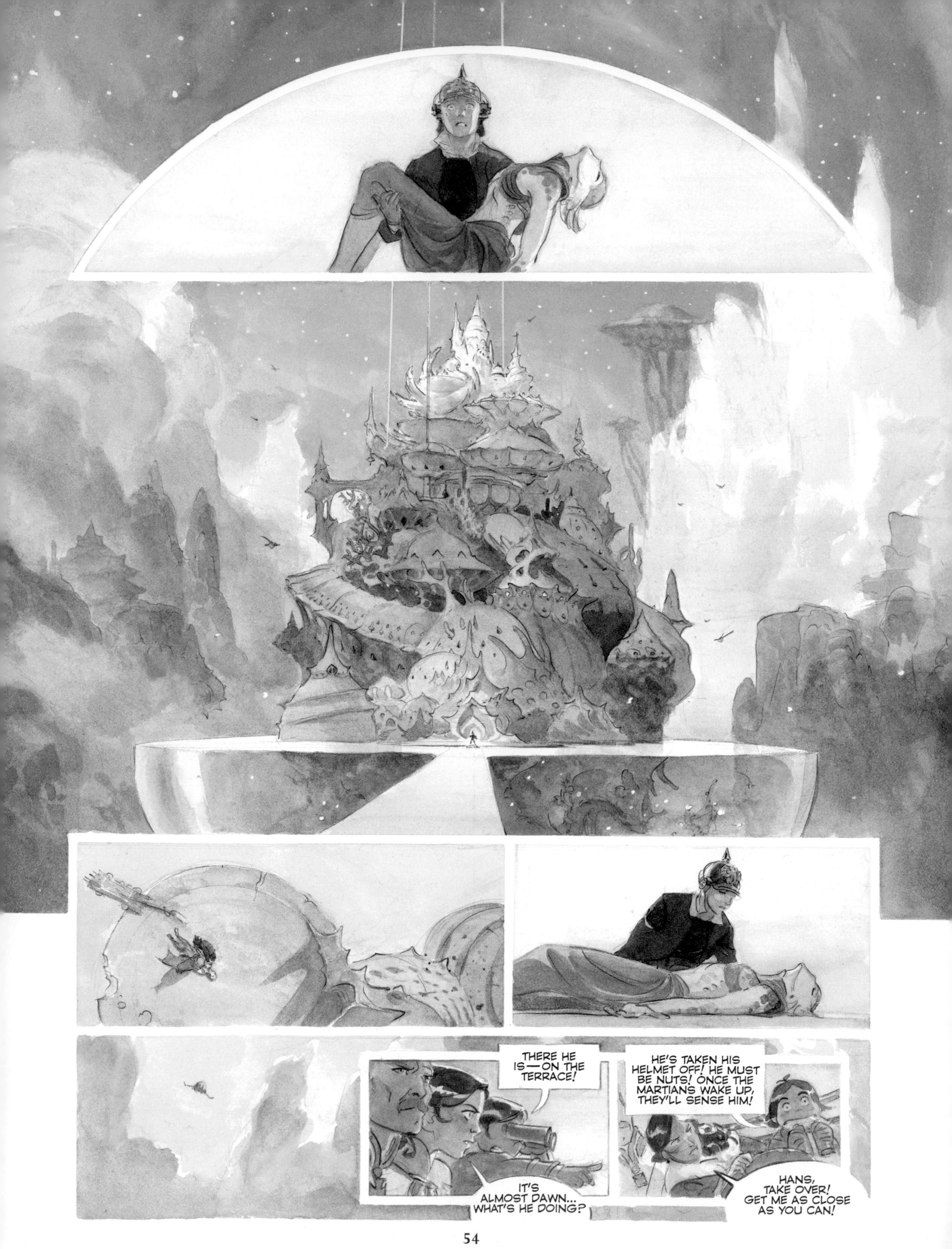

THERE HE IS—ON THE TERRACE!
IT'S ALMOST DAWN... WHAT'S HE DOING?
HE'S TAKEN HIS HELMET OFF! HE MUST BE NUTS! ONCE THE MARTIANS WAKE UP, THEY'LL SENSE HIM!
HANS, TAKE OVER! GET ME AS CLOSE AS YOU CAN!

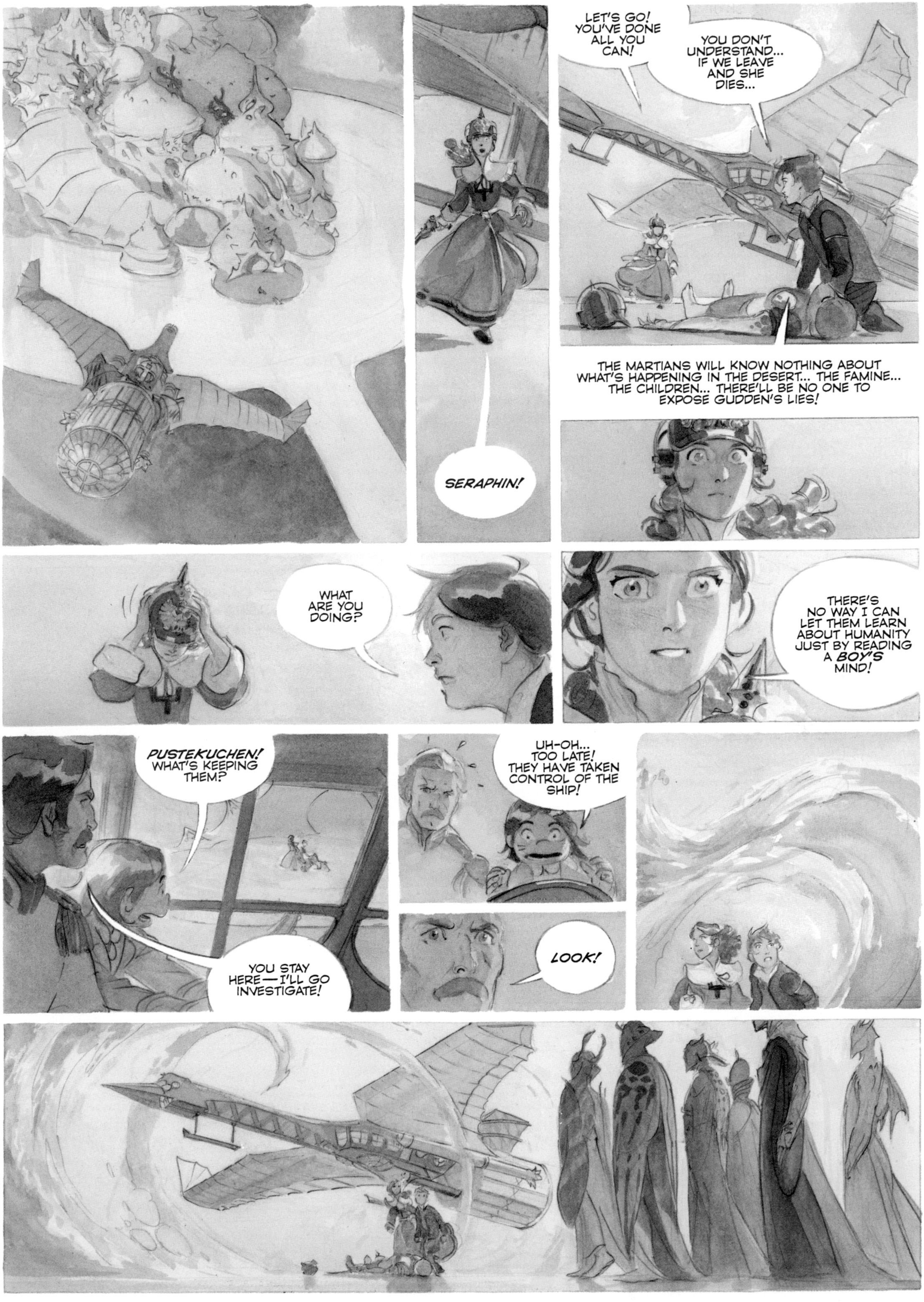
SERAPHIN!
LET'S GO! YOU'VE DONE ALL YOU CAN!
YOU DON'T UNDERSTAND... IF WE LEAVE AND SHE DIES...
THE MARTIANS WILL KNOW NOTHING ABOUT WHAT'S HAPPENING IN THE DESERT... THE FAMINE... THE CHILDREN... THERE'LL BE NO ONE TO EXPOSE GUDDEN'S LIES!
WHAT ARE YOU DOING?
THERE'S NO WAY I CAN LET THEM LEARN ABOUT HUMANITY JUST BY READING A BOY'S MIND!
PUSTEKUCHEN! WHAT'S KEEPING THEM?
YOU STAY HERE—I'LL GO INVESTIGATE!
UH-OH... TOO LATE! THEY HAVE TAKEN CONTROL OF THE SHIP!
LOOK!

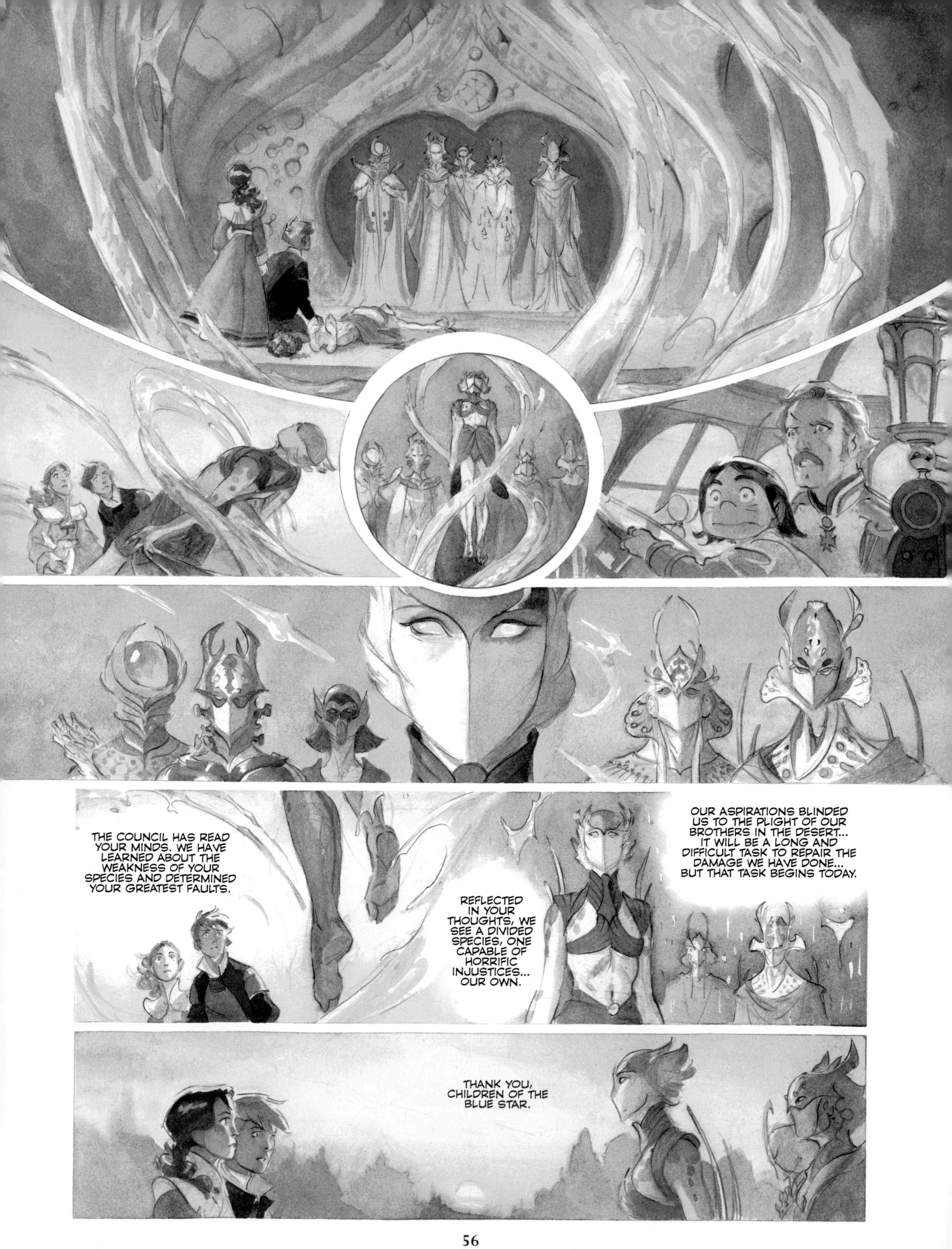
THE COUNCIL HAS READ YOUR MINDS. WE HAVE LEARNED ABOUT THE WEAKNESS OF YOUR SPECIES AND DETERMINED YOUR GREATEST FAULTS.
REFLECTED IN YOUR THOUGHTS, WE SEE A DIVIDED SPECIES, ONE CAPABLE OF HORRIFIC INJUSTICES... OUR OWN.
OUR ASPIRATIONS BLINDED US TO THE PLIGHT OF OUR BROTHERS IN THE DESERT... IT WILL BE A LONG AND DIFFICULT TASK TO REPAIR THE DAMAGE WE HAVE DONE... BUT THAT TASK BEGINS TODAY.
THANK YOU, CHILDREN OF THE BLUE STAR.

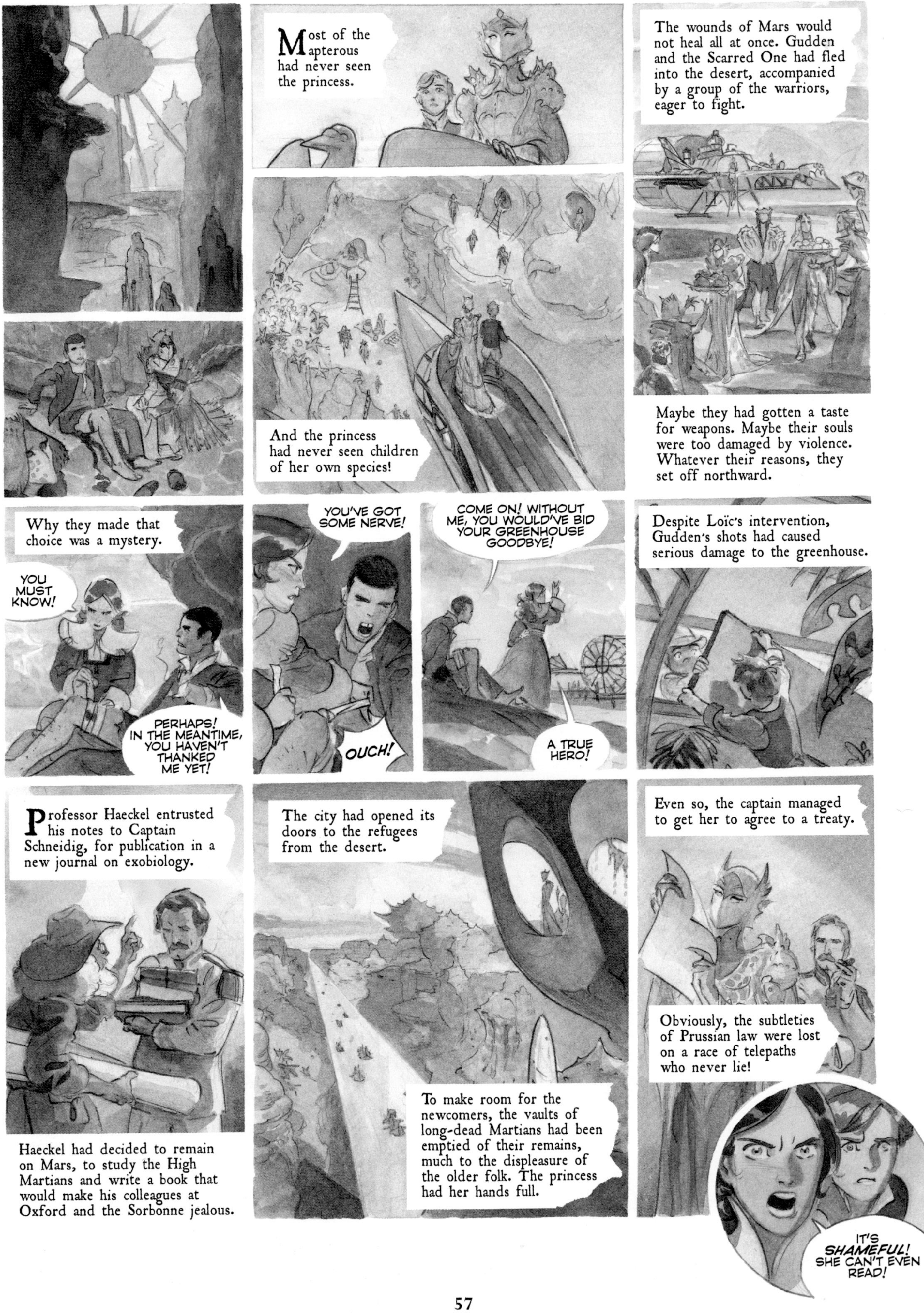
Most of the Mapterous had never seen the princess.
And the princess had never seen children of her own species!
The wounds of Mars would not heal all at once. Gudden and the Scarred One had fled into the desert, accompanied by a group of the warriors, eager to fight.
Maybe they had gotten a taste for weapons. Maybe their souls were too damaged by violence. Whatever their reasons, they set off northward.
Why they made that choice was a mystery.
YOU MUST KNOW!
PERHAPS! IN THE MEANTIME, YOU HAVEN'T THANKED ME YET!
YOU'VE GOT SOME NERVE!
OUCH!
COME ON! WITHOUT ME, YOU WOULD'VE BID YOUR GREENHOUSE GOODBYE!
A TRUE HERO!
Despite Loïc's intervention, Gudden's shots had caused serious damage to the greenhouse.
Professor Haeckel entrusted his notes to Captain Schneidig, for publication in a new journal on exobiology.
Haeckel had decided to remain on Mars, to study the High Martians and write a book that would make his colleagues at Oxford and the Sorbonne jealous.
The city had opened its doors to the refugees from the desert.
To make room for the newcomers, the vaults of long-dead Martians had been emptied of their remains, much to the displeasure of the older folk. The princess had her hands full.
Even so, the captain managed to get her to agree to a treaty.
Obviously, the subtleties of Prussian law were lost on a race of telepaths who never lie!
IT'S SHAMEFUL! SHE CAN'T EVEN READ!

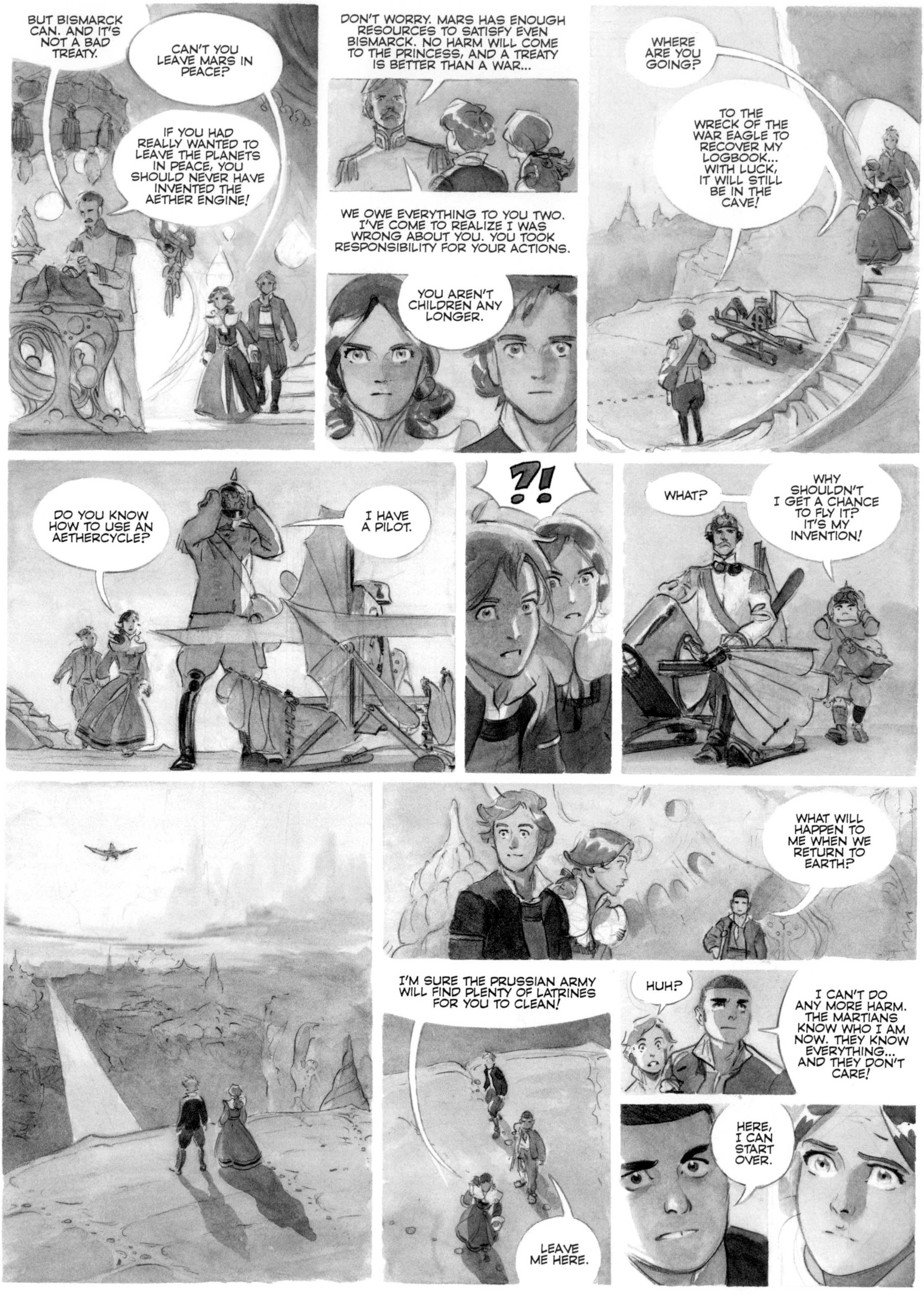
BUT BISMARCK CAN. AND IT'S NOT A BAD TREATY.
CAN'T YOU LEAVE MARS IN PEACE?
IF YOU HAD REALLY WANTED TO LEAVE THE PLANETS IN PEACE, YOU SHOULD NEVER HAVE INVENTED THE AETHER ENGINE!
DON'T WORRY. MARS HAS ENOUGH RESOURCES TO SATISFY EVEN BISMARCK. NO HARM WILL COME TO THE PRINCESS, AND A TREATY IS BETTER THAN A WAR...
WE OWE EVERYTHING TO YOU TWO. I'VE COME TO REALIZE I WAS WRONG ABOUT YOU. YOU TOOK RESPONSIBILITY FOR YOUR ACTIONS.
YOU AREN'T CHILDREN ANY LONGER.
WHERE ARE YOU GOING?
TO THE WRECK OF THE WAR EAGLE TO RECOVER MY LOGBOOK... WITH LUCK, IT WILL STILL BE IN THE CAVE!
DO YOU KNOW HOW TO USE AN AETHERCYCLE?
I HAVE A PILOT.
?!
WHAT?
WHY SHOULDN'T I GET A CHANCE TO FLY IT? IT'S MY INVENTION!
WHAT WILL HAPPEN TO ME WHEN WE RETURN TO EARTH?
I'M SURE THE PRUSSIAN ARMY WILL FIND PLENTY OF LATRINES FOR YOU TO CLEAN!
LEAVE ME HERE.
HUH?
I CAN'T DO ANY MORE HARM. THE MARTIANS KNOW WHO I AM NOW. THEY KNOW EVERYTHING... AND THEY DON'T CARE!
HERE, I CAN START OVER.

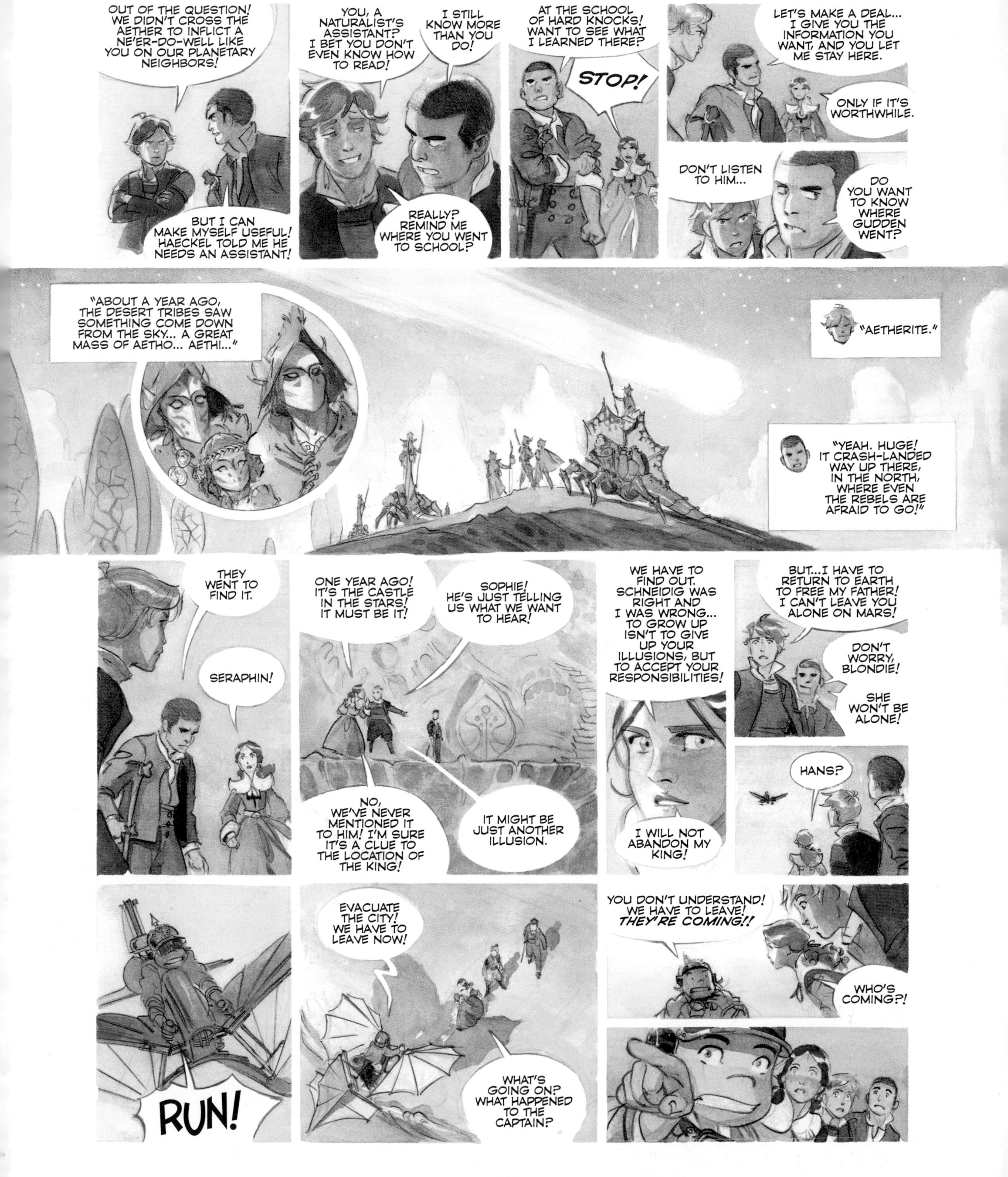

OUT OF THE QUESTION! WE DIDN'T CROSS THE AETHER TO INFLICT A NE'ER-DO-WELL LIKE YOU ON OUR PLANETARY NEIGHBORS!
BUT I CAN MAKE MYSELF USEFUL! HAECKEL TOLD ME HE NEEDS AN ASSISTANT!
YOU, A NATURALIST'S ASSISTANT? I BET YOU DON'T EVEN KNOW HOW TO READ!
I STILL KNOW MORE THAN YOU DO!
REALLY? REMIND ME WHERE YOU WENT TO SCHOOL?
AT THE SCHOOL OF HARD KNOCKS! WANT TO SEE WHAT I LEARNED THERE?
STOP!
LET'S MAKE A DEAL... I GIVE YOU THE INFORMATION YOU WANT, AND YOU LET ME STAY HERE.
ONLY IF IT'S WORTHWHILE.
DON'T LISTEN TO HIM...
DO YOU WANT TO KNOW WHERE GUDDEN WENT?
"ABOUT A YEAR AGO, THE DESERT TRIBES SAW SOMETHING COME DOWN FROM THE SKY... A GREAT MASS OF AETHO... AETHI..."
"AETHERITE."
"YEAH. HUGE! IT CRASH-LANDED WAY UP THERE, IN THE NORTH, WHERE EVEN THE REBELS ARE AFRAID TO GO!"
THEY WENT TO FIND IT.
SERAPHIN!
ONE YEAR AGO! IT'S THE CASTLE IN THE STARS! IT MUST BE IT!
SOPHIE! HE'S JUST TELLING US WHAT WE WANT TO HEAR!
NO, WE'VE NEVER MENTIONED IT TO HIM! I'M SURE IT'S A CLUE TO THE LOCATION OF THE KING!
IT MIGHT BE JUST ANOTHER ILLUSION.
WE HAVE TO FIND OUT. SCHNEIDIG WAS RIGHT AND I WAS WRONG... TO GROW UP ISN'T TO GIVE UP YOUR ILLUSIONS, BUT TO ACCEPT YOUR RESPONSIBILITIES!
I WILL NOT ABANDON MY KING!
BUT...I HAVE TO RETURN TO EARTH TO FREE MY FATHER! I CAN'T LEAVE YOU ALONE ON MARS!
DON'T WORRY, BLONDIE!
SHE WON'T BE ALONE!
HANS?
RUN!
EVACUATE THE CITY! WE HAVE TO LEAVE NOW!
WHAT'S GOING ON? WHAT HAPPENED TO THE CAPTAIN?
YOU DON'T UNDERSTAND! WE HAVE TO LEAVE! THEY'RE COMING!!
WHO'S COMING?!

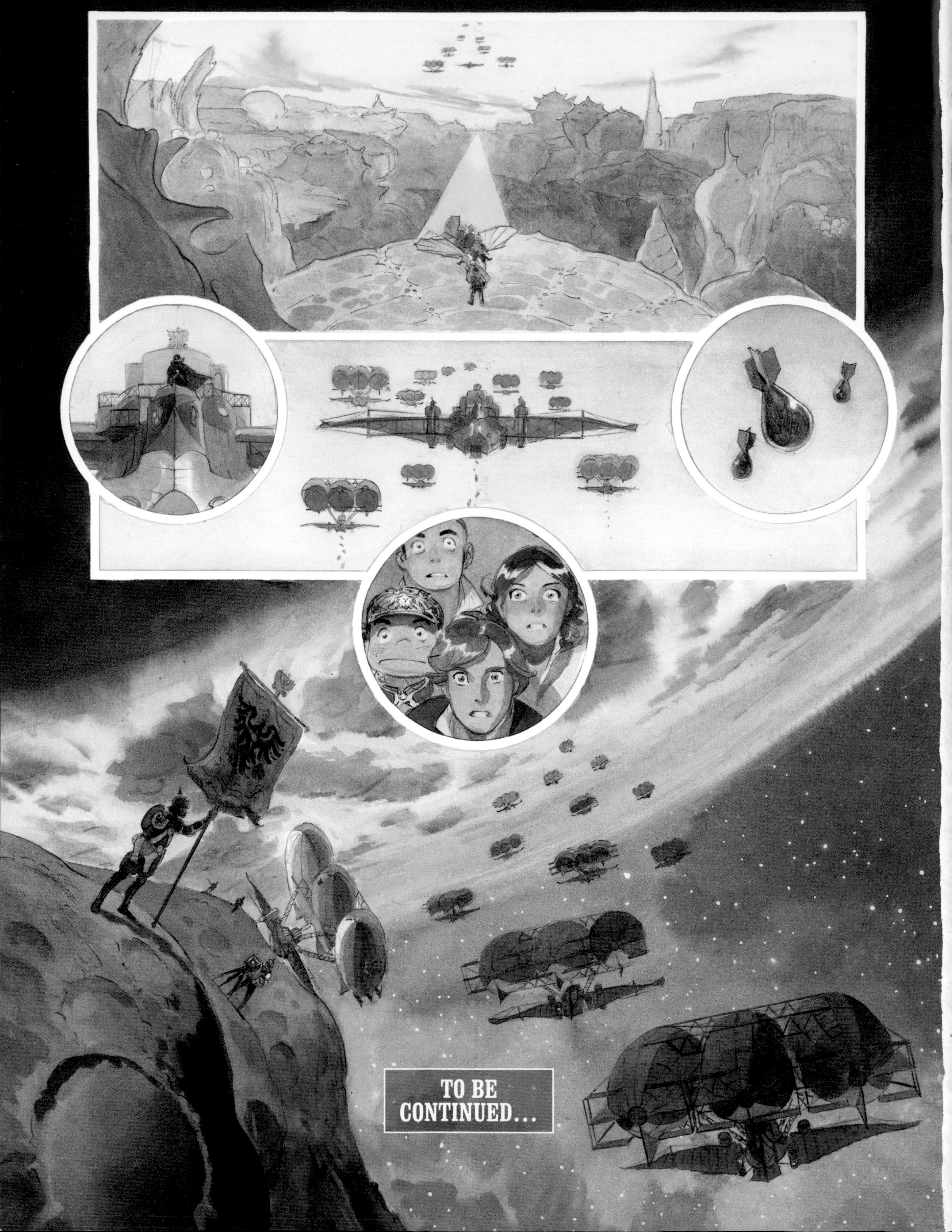
TO BE
CONTINUED...